The Turnpike

Thom Sibbitt

Copyright © 2013 by Thom Sibbitt
Cover art by Megan Thomas
Book design by Thom Sibbitt
All rights reserved.

Printed in the United States of America
First Electronic Edition: January 2013
ISBN-978-0-9887265-1-2

To Hollie, who keeps my stories
and
To Susann, who helps me tell them

Table of Contents

Jumped on Expr.way, hit by truck
I-94 at M-146, Port Huron Twp. MI

*Your pain is the breaking of the shell that
encloses your understanding.*
        —Kahlil Gibran

BLOOD KNOT

There was rain, maybe. Or cool night air with
relentless stars, slightly blurred by the acidic glow of lights over the highway. There
wasn't much confusion or hubbub, perhaps a
young man related the story hours later at a
way station:

A man had fallen from above. He had hit
the hood with great force but strangely little
sound.

Over shaking coffee cups, two or three
wide-eyed strangers nodded their heads and gave
comfort to the driver who killed, no, witnessed
the death of a man who fell from above.

But this comes later…

The time between waking up this morning and sitting on this train has left me feeling shortchanged on comfort and bottlenecked at consciousness. Too many cigarettes last night are not riding well with me.

Gloomy day. A beautiful woman sits across from me. The train is heading underground and my thoughts are happy to submerge with it. Comfort and warmth wait below the surface. The only light is false, fluorescent. Reflections from human-cast lights are crisp and stark, unlike the suspicious grain cast by God's own light. Things exist irrefutably underground. A subway car becomes a display case. Each ear and every glassy curve is in want of ownership.

Lovely woman.

A weary-looking man sits directly across from me. A life of labor. He is no more than a few years older than me, maybe thirty, but no longer young. Life has left dark lines on his face. The tip of his left index finger is a scarred nub. It is a half-inch too short. I imagine his hand mangled in some machine, shock and annoyance on his face.

He is probably hungry. Always. And every Lilith who crosses his view puts another year of age under his eyes.

Contact.

Our eyes touch for just a moment and I see something more vulnerable than his appearance would suggest. Something rises to my throat. I shift my gaze and catch my reflection in the plastic window over his shoulder. My cocky English greatcoat and my thinning pompadour expose something desperate about me. I look away.

Lovely woman.

The train shudders on the tracks. The passengers on board sway in time with the

movement. We are all held inside a train
that's making love roughly to the steel rails.
The rhythm lulls my mind into a moment of
stillness.

The muscles in that man's neck scream for
open sky.

From the early morning fog, a solitary motorcycle emerges on an almost lost highway…

I come out of the subway around Grand Central Station. As I walk, I see glimpses of a white sun rising between passing side streets. New York is more beautiful than ever, cold and Decembery. Corridors of stalwart brick crouch below cliff faces of white concrete. A flashy cornice of the Chrysler Building catches a bit of the morning sun and lights up like a divine turn signal. The beauty of this moment catches me. A sudden surge of happiness crawls warmly around in my bowels and lurks up into the corners of my mouth. Today is anything. Today is everything.

Inhaling, I turn my head back to the street just in time to see a young kid staring from a taxicab window. He is in the backseat alone. His expression is drawn and tight, some powerful grief.

I watch as the cab pulls up to the corner across from where I'm standing. The boy is quite young, not more than ten. He reaches into his navy blue blazer, pulls out a few bills, and pays the driver.

Entranced, I watch as he gets out of the cab. He checks his wristwatch, slings a backpack over his shoulder, walks deliberately through revolving doors, and vanishes into the lobby of a midtown high-rise.

I imagine this young boy is the CEO of a company on his way to a board meeting. He will have to make some big layoffs after the drop this quarter.

I shake my head in spite of myself and continue walking up the avenue. I am grateful not to have been raised in the city.

Omaha. Homaha.

It's funny that while the dreams and expectations of my parents crumbled, my childhood remains porcelain and magical, at least in my mind. I remember picturesque Fourth of Julys, with fireflies dancing voluptuously in the backyard. I remember my father's scraggly mouth twisting into a rare and beautiful smile. By the time I was eighteen, however, I ran screaming from my hometown.

My father died when I was ten. It was the very same day there was a bird plague in Illinois. I wasn't there, but I heard birds were falling off trees and wires like heavy walnuts.

Crossing the street, I approach a coffee cart and decide a coffee will be good. The man running the cart is sporting a thick mustache and smiles as I walk up.

-Morning, boss.

-Regular please, I respond, and please don't call me boss, I say with a smile.

He looks up with a slightly perturbed expression.

-Sure thing, boss. OK.

He smiles, handing me the coffee and holding his hand out for money. I stand there looking at his well-picked-through selection of doughnuts. Nothing strikes my fancy, so I dig into my pocket, pull out a dollar, and place it into his outstretched hand.

-Thanks, boss.

-No problem, I say, keep the change.

His smile turns into a scowl as I walk away and I can hear him muttering under his breath.

Why did I say that? Lighting up a cigarette I continue to walk, feeling like that exchange was far too antagonistic for street coffee. Hostility and politeness intertwined, inviting us both to bare our teeth, come to blows, draw blood.

Keep the change? I think.

-Don't say that again, I say aloud, which immediately draws the attention of an old woman walking a Schnauzer wearing a doggy Christmas sweater alongside of me. She throws me a sharp glance and shakes her head in disapproval. The Schnauzer chortles.

I guess I'm this morning's sideshow. Suddenly I stop. It feels like there is something descending down on top of me. Revolving doors. Stale donuts. Schnauzers.

Taking a drag from my cigarette, I pull the smoke deep into my lungs, trying to resettle. A bench is invitingly nestled in a nook of wrought iron on the outside perimeter of Bryant Park. It is down the street a ways, so I start to jog toward it, afraid someone might take up residence before I can get there.

Hot coffee sloshes out of my cup and splashes onto my wrist. People swarm around the bench as if they are taunting me, daring me to sit there before them. As I get close, I slow down to a stroll, trying to appear uninterested in the bench, while wiping coffee away from my wrist with the sleeve of my coat. I am there and sit unchallenged.

My cigarette has become a worthless wet butt, so I light another and sink deeply into the bench. Getting from A to B in this city is difficult and I don't really know where I am going. I thought I would just get off the train somewhere and walk. Pedestrians pass by me in a steady stream with little apparent difficulty. They are on their way. Purposeful. Ambitious.

My head is spinning slowly. City vertigo. In spite of the dull pain, I find the sensation calming, like a shot of whiskey. I close my eyes and let the sounds and the smells of the city fill me.

The wood of my bench smells vaguely of a Greyhound bus. My grandfather took me to the bus station when I first left home. He gave me a brown paper bag filled with oranges and oatmeal cookies. In the station he made me swear, in all seriousness, that leaving for New York did not mean I was joining the army. I must not join the army under any circumstances.

I perfunctorily made my promise, got on the bus, entering into a smell much like this city park bench: sweet perspiration, vague bleach, overripe soggy newspaper. Intoxicated with expectation, I glanced out the window to see my grandfather standing under a stuttering fluorescent light, wringing his brown winter fedora in his hands. I was offended by his lack of enthusiasm or pride in my boldness. I barely gave notice to the lines of grief surrounding his frustrated eyes until this moment.

On a musty New York City bench, a vision comes to me, an uncovered memory of my grandfather neither waving nor shedding a tear, but struggling to hold still his body from trembling with sorrow. At the time, I simply waved from my fogged window and sunk back into my pungent seat, fascinated by the sensation of walking up to a precipice and diving off.

A large garbage truck stops just in front of me and breaks my meditation. Here I am, at the bottom of the precipice. It stinks. The garbage truck noisily ambles down the street. A mob of people swiftly walk in a chaotic swarm just inches from me. My park bench sanctuary was a bed for someone last night. My coffee has grown cold. John Lennon is nowhere to be seen. He hasn't been seen on these streets for twenty years.

My morning stroll is over. I stand up and start walking back toward the subway. Back underground.

Another motorcycle comes whizzing by from the direction the rider is headed. The other biker is coming out of a rainy patch, dressed in a bright yellow rain suit. They both raise their gloved hands in encouragement. Though the fog has burned off with the afternoon sun, soggy clouds still drag across the country. Rain ahead. The Rider decides it is time to pull over and put on his own bright yellow rain suit.

Home. Standing in the center of my Brooklyn studio, I try to decide where to hang this string of Christmas lights. I saw lights strung in the window of the deli between my apartment and the train station. They looked festive and I thought a little Christmas spirit might lighten my world up a bit, so I bought a box and brought them home.

I consider stringing them around my bed like erotic limelights. The image of myself as a burnt corpse, however, smiling up at the ceiling, quickly puts me off the idea. My other options are a window, my bookshelf, or the doorway to the bathroom. This is the extent of my studio, so the placement deserves serious consideration.

The bookshelf, I decide. I use tape from my desk and start hanging the lights back and forth across the shelves. Titles are illuminated when I plug in the string of lights: *Sentimental Education*, *Hunger*, *Tropic of Cancer*, *The Most Beautiful Girl in Town*. Each book is an inviting escape hatch, a five-by-nine ripcord with rescue parachute attached.

A book is tempting right now, something to settle my mind, but I step away from the shelf and look at my handiwork. With the lights up, the rest of my apartment actually looks inviting. On my desk there are a few pictures, a postcard of the mountains where my father's ashes were spread and a picture of my grandmother. The rest of the clutter is unopened junk mail and stacks of abandoned writing projects piled around a hand-me-down desktop computer.

Otherwise, there are four bare walls, a cracked and uneven ceiling, and two drafty windows that look out onto the train platform. Nestled behind my landlord's garage, my room is on the ground floor. It is quiet and private, which is no more or less than I need.

16

Outside it has begun to snow. The flakes are thick and fluffy and give no sign of letting up anytime soon.

Sitting down at my desk, I power up the computer. The silence of my room is broken by the whirr of the hard drive warming up. The old PC takes time to boot up; I sit patiently while it makes tiny popcorn noises and the screen flickers to life.

I open a new Word document. The cursor blinks tauntingly on a screen that is otherwise all white. The page is waiting to be filled with a poem or a story. Anything. A word. I could use a Sharpie pen and draw a smiley face on the screen. That would be something, but my mind is a blank reflection of the white page. I have nothing to say.

I open my e-mail, but there is only piece of spam and a reminder that I've not made a payment on my student loan and my credit is at risk.

I could call someone. Frank invited me over for dinner again, but I'm not hungry. I could call my sister, but I'm afraid I would just be a bummer. I could call my ex-girlfriend and see if she will talk with me, but that would probably just be mean. I was an asshole to her.

What do I want?

My mind remains as blank as the screen. Maybe I can relax if I masturbate. I know better and I am not really in the mood, but what else am I going to do?

I unzip my pants and hold my flaccid penis in my hand. Massaging it does nothing, so I put my elbow on my desk and navigate to a free porn site. There are thirty-second clips in low resolution. Not much for quality, but there are hundreds, thousands, of clips. There must be something here that can turn me on.

The rain is coming in waves now. Thoughts of shelter pass like mailboxes on the road.

Where am I going? he asks himself.

I am going to die out here on this little bike. He shakes that nagging thought away. It is nice to be out on the road again, even in the rain.

His thoughts continue to accumulate darkness as the patchy clouds and the starless black sky cools the air around him. On a bike, you can feel the tiniest changes in temperature. If you drive past a house in the summer, where some golfer is watering his lawn, you feel the air change as you fly by. The moisture is gripping and clings to you. And smells are heightened: water on cement, cut grass, roadkill, or a silky perfume slipping out of a passing car with its windows rolled down for the breeze.

He is both exhilarated and miserable in the light rain. The chill pushes him past his tolerance of discomfort while giving him a constant reminder that he is very much alive. It's the misery that comes in exchange for the euphoria of shifting up into fifth gear out on the plains and having the bike just float off the ground.

I'm seeing spots. It has grown dark outside.
I don't know what I am looking for, but hours
have passed and I've not cum. I look down at
my dick. It is still hard but looks pathetic
sticking out of my jeans crookedly and cradled
in my hand.

-What am I doing? I say aloud.

A screen full of contorted women look back
at me with an indifferent hum. I feel cheated.
My evening is gone. I'm starving. I've done
nothing and I feel chained to this chair
because I've not yet cum.

My sex drive has probably prevented me from
being an astronaut or a senator. I could have
been this writer-savant-manchild. Instead, I
have stuffed landfills with cum-stained tissues.

This is not enough. It is never enough. I
reach up and turn the computer off. It lets out
a disappointed fading buzz and then the room is
silent again.

I rub my eyes with my free hand and use
the other to put my fading penis back into my
pants.

I am hungry, but don't want to eat. Hunger,
at least, I can feel.

About the room, everything sits quietly.
It is like being ignored. This is my room. My
desk. My books. My wallet on the counter. My
dishes. They have no right to ignore me.

Standing, I take a few steps to the full-
length mirror hanging on my bathroom door. What
I see surprises me. I look like my mother, from
a rare picture of her kept by my grandfather.
In the picture my mother had a Tinkerbelle
haircut, held her arms above her head, and was
laughing like one of the Lost Boys.

My face is still freshly shaven. When my
beard reaches a certain length I see my father

staring back at me and I usually shave it immediately.

I've never seen my mother in the mirror before. Maybe I wasn't looking. She is a drug-addicted, paranoid schizophrenic who spent weekends with me as a small child telling me that my father was a closet homosexual, that he'd been gang raped, was a drunk, etc.... I was too young to understand what she meant, but who wants to look into the mirror and see that? I haven't talked to her in years.

But there she is, standing in the mirror before me. I see her wild eyes and her cheeks and her boyish light brown hair.

She holds out her hand to me. A small gesture. An invitation. As if she wants me to step through the mirror into a labyrinth beyond. Through passageways and pitfalls she will be there, waiting for me. My minotaur.

I shake my head and she disappears. I watched too much TV as a child. The next thing I know David Bowie is going to step out of my bathroom juggling peaches.

For a moment, I consider punching my fist through the mirror. I imagine the glass cutting into my fingers.

I am hungry. My irises are fucked.

I will have horrible dreams.

White light. Bed Spins. Eyelids fluttering. Eyes rolling deeply back into their sockets.

Arms strapped. Legs. Head bound.

Gray, nonanatomical shapes floating through space, breaking up the holy white light.

Hands grip and release. A cry peels out from tightened cords, to become entangled in foamy light.

Eyes closed and journey backward to before.

White turns into red oxygen rich blood seeping from gravel scraped knee.

The street is empty, save for a dingy brown cat.

Cries fill the open spaces and bounce off empty porches to echo back unanswered.

(This is before the tying of the blood knot.)

Until a screen door wails in its opening and barks in its slamming shut. Heavy legs lumber across unkempt grass toward the crying and bloody knee.

Socks slip down the thudding calves, as a grandmother in skirts and torn sweater and braided hair hunkers down next to the child.

Dabbing with wet cloth. Humming from the throat through closed lips. Swaying mother's mother's mother and stranger too.

Cry subsides and breathing is an audible gasp.

—Dance the pain dance, my darling. What does it do?

Intrepid girl. Shaking and suddenly adrift. Uncovers the wound. Raises arms skyward with glistening stigmata, drying in the wind. Stands and sways in time with her own heartbeats.

Blood trickles in a single droplet down the shin, to be gobbled up by a high white sock.

—Good, my sweetheart. Dance with me. Do the blood dance.

They sway in the empty street, watched by curtained windows and flagged mailboxes.

A child with marionette arms raised overhead and grandmother sunk in on her haunches swaying to the heartbeats.

TROUBLED HEDGEROWS

I can't sleep. The room stinks of cigarettes
and my bed is starting to suffocate me. For
the last couple of hours I've been lying here
staring into the darkness of my room. Every
twenty minutes or so I can hear the train roll
over the platform and stop at the station on
the corner. I've tried counting the number
of trains as they passed, but I cannot stay
focused and keep having to start over after the
third train.

The bars will be open until 4:00 a.m. I
consider grabbing a drink, but I don't even
know what time it is. My mind is flatlining.
Nothing is bothering me. Nothing is nagging,
but I might as well be trying to sleep on top
of a subway car.

I kick my feet out of the bed and stand
naked in the center of my room. The air is cold
outside of the blankets, but it feels good.
In a moment I am dressed and tightening the
laces of my shoes. I am not going to a bar.

That would not end well. The snow has stopped falling so I will walk until my body says stop.

Outside the streets are empty. Anyone not in bed at this time of night either is up to no good or is very foolish. It is too cold tonight to be anything other than foolish.

At the corner, I turn right and walk below the train tracks down the avenue. A red car is parked in the center of the empty lot of the middle school. Inside the car is a man wearing a rumpled orange coat. I cannot tell if he is sleeping or awake. I imagine he is looking through his window staring at me.

I quicken my pace and stare ahead, as if I am heading somewhere. My heart is racing. It feels good.

The train screeches in the distance. It is coming around a bend in the tracks in my direction. The noise is somewhat muted by the new snow but still rattles my teeth. The train rumbles above me as I shuffle beneath it trying to ignore the noise. Everything is shaking in the cacophony. The vibration travels through the concrete and up through my shoes. It shakes my kneecaps and travels into my cold thighs.

Over my shoulder, I see a few people stiffly marching down the steps of the train platform. I've no idea what time it is. They are probably the last crowd arriving home from the bars this evening.

I turn my attention forward again and continue down the street. From ahead of me an old white Cadillac is trolling toward me. It is captained by an extremely fat man with a bald head. The car slows almost to a stop as it closes in on me and the fat man gives me a little honk.

He stares imploringly through the window at me, hoping I will turn a trick or something for him, I suppose. My eyes remain fixed on the sidewalk, however, and the Cadillac keeps rolling down the street. I don't want to look back lest I give the wrong impression, so I turn the corner and begin to circle the block.

I bumped into a hooker on this street one evening a few weeks back. I'd seen her around the neighborhood several times before. She always wears the same black Adidas jacket, no matter what the weather is, and she smells of dirt and very strong cheap perfume. I remember as I walked past her she asked me if I liked the scent. I told her I thought it was lovely. She smiled at me.

I must not have given her the impression that I was the "John" type. We just made small talk for a few minutes. She asked me my name and I told her. She said her name was Gina and that her sister was a famous actor on television.

She had thick fingers, like a mechanic's. During the day I've seen her collecting cans. At night she is usually strolling beneath the train tracks trying to flag down cars.

It is a strange thing to make conversation with a woman who has dick on her breath. I didn't find that it made her any less charming, though.

The cold is starting to get to me. I don't think I'd mind bumping into Gina tonight. The thought makes my heart race slightly. I scan the empty streets for someone, but tonight there is no one left walking but me.

This feeling of anticipation rises into my throat and tightens. I've seen several women walking these streets and never given it much thought. I see a transsexual woman out here regularly making rounds. She scares the shit out of me because when she looks at me she seems to recognize me and stares as if she is about to steal my lunch money.

There is also a flamboyant black woman who is always wearing a tattered gray sweater. She has a garrulous smile and a habit of singing to herself. She looks like a real hustler and gives the impression of loving her work.

I ask myself every time I see her, what is a person made of who is totally fearless of the night? I imagine her offering the Grim Reaper a blow job on the way down to hell. The thought makes me smile in spite of myself.

A feeling of innocent helplessness fills me as I continue to roam the empty street. When I left my apartment my mind was blank and my chest was still.

Now my heart is pounding in my chest. I could bump into someone out here and anything could happen. I could be predator or prey. I would welcome it.

But nothing happens and I just walk and walk and walk.

Streetlights blink. Train cars rumble. There is no one on these streets but me. Time to head home. Maybe I am off the hook tonight. Maybe I am still on it. I don't think I care. I just can't help thinking that walking out here is close to feeling alive. I like it.

His worry grows as he passes one sleepy town after the next. The rain had ebbed a little, making room for dense cool air to settle about his ankles. The highway is a misty wormhole through his headlight.

Questions cycle through his mind.

Where the hell am I? How long have I been driving? Where am I going? What I am going to do?

Bothersome questions pile up with the miles and amount to very little. He looks forward. Only forward, down the road.

MARATHON

POPULATION 287

Another town, sleep soon maybe. He drops his speed and tries to loosen his limbs. His hands clutch the handgrips. He stretches his legs, and this sends a shiver down his knees all the way to his toes. The cold is becoming unbearable.

-I've got to get off this damn thing, he says inside his helmet.

The words fog his visor; he cracks it open, letting the cool air onto his face and neck.

The shape of a few single story buildings and driveways begin to materialize. This town is small, not even a gas station. He downshifts as his eyes refocus from the black panorama onto vague shapes and lights.

The warm neon of a roadside café beckons, and across the street in the periphery of its glow, another motorcyclist idles. The motorcycle is a big one. A hog. As modest as chrome can be under the lamplight.

In the cold, the town and the Harley roll up
so fast he begins to panic, thinking he might
just drive on by. His body works down through
the gears—*easy on those brakes*—and a shaky, if
not bold slide alongside of the-bike-so-much-
bigger.

She's a woman. It's a surprise that almost
slips out of his mouth. She is wrapped up in
rich leathers. Over the rumble of the bikes he
croaks out,

-Ah...yeah. How's it going? Do you know if
there is a campground anywhere near by?

She takes him in. He watches her take him
in. She is about the same age as his sister,
One-Punch Paula (her biker name). Biker names
always have such flare: "Double D." "New York
Slick." "J.C."

Like his sister, this woman gives the
impression of once being the jewel of this
small town. The beauty still lives in her eyes.

In that shared moment of idling and evening
wind, the door to the café across the street
swings open and a boy about fourteen, in full
football regalia—pads, cleats, gray pants and a
red jersey—steps out onto the gravel entryway.
The boy jogs across the street, gives the
strange rider a long look through his headgear,
and then leaps nimbly onto the back of his
mother's motorcycle.

-Well, she says abruptly, why don'tcha follow
me down the road aways? We'll go ask the Old
Man. With that, she gasses the throttle and
thunders down the road.

-Wow. The thought escapes his lips, but his
body is slow to follow.

He watches the taillight of the big
motorcycle as the woman and her son begin
to disappear down the road ahead of him. He
snaps to attention and throws his bike into

gear. With a pull of the throttle, his little motorcycle zips down the road after her.

-Wake up! A voice cuts into the darkness.

A rough shake brings my startled mind back to life. The glare of fluorescent subway lights pinches my retina. My hand comes up to my eyes as if to rub away the rough light.

I'm on the train again. Going nowhere. I must have fallen asleep. A huge man is standing over me with a blank look on his face. His hand still clutches my shoulder.

-You were yelling, he says.

-What?

-Yelling, man. You were yelling in your sleep.

With that he lets go of my arm and sits back down on the bench across from me.

Still confused, I sit up and look around the train. The car is empty except for me and this big man who just woke me up.

I was yelling? I wonder what I was yelling. I want to ask him, but I suppose if it was enough for him to decide to shake me awake, it was probably not a pretty sight.

It's awkward, suddenly, with just him and me on the train, sitting across from each other. The train stops at the next station, the doors open, but no one else gets in. We both shift in our seats uneasily and look at the doors, and then not back at each other, then back to the ground between us.

He is a big guy. His face is scarred and heavy. His cheeks are long and somnolent with large lips he keeps slightly open, as if it is too much work to keep them closed. His eyelids are impossibly large and sad.

We are the same age, or close. We probably live in the same neighborhood. I can tell he is going nowhere and the weight of that is plain in his eyes. The train lurches suddenly, then resettles back on the tracks. He lays his head back against the window and sighs. Most people would consider him ugly, but I think he is beautiful. The impossibility of enduring life with a face like that and the deadpan reflection of those rough lines in his face cuts right through the center of my chest. My clean face grows whiter and something ugly inside of me tightens. He suddenly looks at me.

It only lasts a moment and he regards the anxiety in my eyes with a smile, or at least the possibility of one. Then he lays his head back against the rattling window and I do the same.

My studio is bleak and isolated. The white Christmas lights hung around my bookshelf fill the room with a nostalgic aura. I'm sitting on my bed with my hand down my pants, enjoying a sensation of irony. I'm losing control of something. Getting up, I stand in front of the mirror with my dick out, watching it grow. There is a fire behind my eyes. A dull pinch hits the back of my heart. It flickers like a matador's cape.

I begin to pace back and forth in my room. I think again that it is time to call Frank. I need to get out of this apartment, but the idea of sitting around talking about art or life just makes me want to rage.

I could just go to Big Lights, the bar I work at, and hang out there. My friend J.B. will feed me drinks all night. Kylie and the other bartenders will flirt with me. Hell, I might even get laid.

I start to put on some clothes. I am sitting on my bed tying my shoes, and I am filled with this unmistakable feeling that I am being watched. Something catches my eye and I turn my head quickly to the mirror across the room.

I am there in the reflection, tying up my shoes. What I see is nothing special, just a guy with jeans on and a faded T-shirt. Nonetheless, I am arrested by what I see. Everything about me is together and in its place, but there is a hot aura around me, like a meteor entering the atmosphere with chunks flying off of it.

-What? I ask. What the fuck do you want?

No answer. And suddenly it comes clear. I am not going to the bar. I am not calling Frank. I want to destroy something.

A thought rises to the surface and I see that same image of my mother again, with her wild eyes. Her hand is outstretched and beckoning for me to step through the glass into the dark world beyond. Her face is almost loving, full of maniacal laughter. She is a child running through dimly lit city streets, daring and absolutely free.

My mind bends around the image. She is not there. There is only me, in the midst of tying my shoes. Perhaps I am going crazy. Perhaps I will spend the rest of my life, like my mother, sedated in a ward.

I want to stifle this growing sense of panic. I want to calm my nerves by experiencing some sense of feeling or connection. I want to feel alive.

I look into the mirror. Through the glass I imagine myself as an animal, prowling in a dark land. I stalk prey through perilous brambles. I must kill to survive. I see a doe drinking water from an oily pond. In a bloodlust, I pounce and hungrily begin to devour its flesh. I do not notice the hunter that steps from the shadows behind me. The figure does not hesitate. With surgical clarity, a knife is run across my gut and my bowels drop onto the ground before me. All that I have devoured lays at my feet. With an irresistible starvation, I begin to scoop up my entrails in my hands and begin to feed once more. I will be forced to dine again and again.

I shake this image from my head. This has to stop. My mouth is agape and the laces of my right shoe dangle limply from my fingertips. Forgetting the laces, I stand and walk to the mirror.

Avoiding looking at my reflection, I place my hands on the sides of the mirror and attempt to pull it from the door. Four small plastic brackets hold it in place. I pull and the mirror begins to bend in its center, threatening to shatter.

That's the last thing I need.

I swipe the stapler off my desk and use it like a hammer to pound on one of the brackets. It won't budge.

Frustrated now, I pull the stapler back and swing it down hard. The bracket explodes and the stapler slips off to the side, smashing my finger onto the glass. Yelping, I drop the stapler to the floor, hop up and down, and wave my hand in the air.

My pointer finger is red, and there is already a faint blue color rising under the nail, but the mirror is unmarred. With a deep breath I take a last look into the mirror. Eyes. Nose. Mouth. It will be nice to forget this face for a while.

Gently, I pull the mirror loose from the last three brackets. Careful not to drop it or bang the glass into my table, I crouch down next to my bed and slide the mirror lengthwise under the bed frame.

A relieved sigh escapes from my mouth. I sit on the bed and finish tying my shoe, trying not to use my now throbbing finger. I must go for a walk. Then I might be able to relax, even sleep.

The door leading outside of my apartment looms with a sense of foreboding and excitement. The door almost vibrates with anticipation. I stand and open it.

There will be no rest. In sleep or wake.

The rider rolls onto the driveway of an ancient farmhouse. There is a big garage, and in the fuzzy porch light a lush green lawn stretches into the darkness. Four or five children quickly emerge from the shadows. Whether these are neighborhood kids or all from the womb of this...woman, is hard to tell. One child, clearly the leader, steps forward.

This portly boy is neither the smallest nor the biggest but is somehow already affecting some male pattern balding. The fat boy introduces himself as soon as both bikes are turned off. Over the clicking of the cooling engines he extends a grubby paw and shakes the cold, gloved hand of the rider and gives him a toothy, infectious grin.

-Mister, the name is Bill, but they call me Fart.

The older boy in the football garb walks past Fart with a grunt but says nothing. His cleats click against the concrete driveway and up a wooden porch covered in flaking green paint that leads into the house.

It is impossible not to smile.

With a *Shoooo!* the apparent mother of this shoeless gaggle ushers the rider through the curious stares of the wild children and into the old house.

The porch opens into the kitchen and inside there are two teenage girls. They're already beautiful, with sharp eyes and long braided hair. The girls are in the middle of cleaning up a failed dinner. A plate piled with burnt hamburgers, still raw in the middle, has been discarded on the counter.

The woman of the house points to the kitchen table, a sign for the rider to sit and make himself not quite comfortable, and then speaks.

-The Old Man just got off work, so he is

still in the shower. You just sit there and warm yourself. The girls didn't do so good with dinner, so we'll see about that later.

She disappears down a hallway, and the rider is left for a moment with a kitchen full of rug rats. The house is big, but it isn't rich. It's full of old things: empty birdcages, long beaded curtains, and countless mismatched sneakers. The home is lived in. Smoke clings in the stained corners of the dark walls.

The kids, led by Fart, are full of questions and jokes. Fart doesn't hesitate to unpack his whole routine of farting on command, which he calls his fart machine, followed by his delivery of flawless Rodney Dangerfield impressions. His charisma has clearly earned him much respect among the youngsters. The rider sits and smiles at the children. The warmth of the home and the eager children envelop him. His body begins to loosen up after the chilly evening ride.

Suddenly a voice booms over the laughter of the children crowded in the kitchen.

-Fart! Give it a rest with that poop machine of yours!

And from the beaded doorway emerges the not-so-old Old Man. He is huge. He carries a tremendous belly, and a stark footlong goateed chin juts from his otherwise bald head. He is naked except for a pair of tight yellow sweat shorts and a cigarette.

Old Man stands in the doorway and sizes up the awkward young rider, who has a growing self-consciousness about his clean-cut face and English-style black leather jacket.

-Looks like my Old Lady brought home another man. What's your name, son? The big man asks between long pulls at his smoke.

With a cough the young man replies,

-Well, sir, my name is Tom.

This elicits a grunt from the big man.

-Don't call me sir. The name is Ray, but friends call me Titan. Looks like you've met my wife. She's Old Lady. I guess these kids are ours. The stinky one is Fart. The rest of 'em got names too.

With another quick glance at young master Fart, the worried rider named Tom realizes that Titan and his son Fart are the spitting image of each other.

On the street. Snow is beginning to fall from between the tracks above me. It falls onto the sleeping row houses, all lined with festive lights. The homes seem to welcome passersby from the street. Lighting up a cigarette, I turn my head forward and quicken my pace. The sidewalk is covered in ice and my toes are already getting cold. For a moment I consider turning around and going back into my apartment. I should just jerk off and go to sleep. My feet are clinging to the sidewalk like fingers in the hand strap of a subway car. Even in the heavy silence of the snow-covered roofs, it feels like I am standing in the middle of a department store with crying children, and complaining shoppers, and registers moaning with the weight of holiday bonuses and rubbery credit cards. I walk faster. I look down the side streets. When I bring the cigarette to my mouth again, my hand is shaking inside my glove. I am not cold. I just hate myself. I hate this.

I stop. My breath hangs in the air in front of me. Through my frost-dragon breath I see Gina, pacing under a streetlight to stay warm. She sees me and she smiles. I say nothing. I just turn around and start walking back to my apartment, knowing she will follow. I hear her slipping on the ice behind me, trying to catch up, but I do not slow down. I walk faster, almost running away from her. As I turn the corner back to my street she catches up with me.

-Hey, she says.

-Hey.

A cop car rolls by slowly as we as duck down the drive and go into my apartment where it is warm and the dainty lights await.

Before she leaves I make her a cup of coffee
and she asks me if I have any loose change.
I tell her no, but I give her all the empty
beer bottles I have in the place. We don't
say anything when she leaves. The door closes
against a gust of wind and I sit alone again
on my bed. My mind has stopped, but my heart
continues to race. I open the fridge and take
out a beer. It is time to drink. I should sleep
now but I am not tired. The room still smells
like street grime and oily perfume. I smell my
hands and frown. Another beer.

I go to the sink and wash my hands and then
sit down at my computer screen. I got this
computer from Frank as a hand-me-down after
college. He got a new laptop and I inherited
this old thing. I thought it would be good for
writing, but I mostly use it to look at porn on
the Internet. The computer is old and slow. It
makes waiting for pictures of naked women to
upload very laborious. I sit there for maybe an
hour. I look at naked teens. I look at black
women and Asian women. I look at older women
getting gang banged. I look at a girl who looks
like my ex-girlfriend getting her face fucked
until she gags and starts to cry and eventually
vomits up semen and what looks like blood. In
the last picture she looks happy. She smiles.

I turn off my computer. I zip up my pants. I
wrap my hands around the monitor and I lift it
off the desk. It is connected to the wall and
the hard drive tower, but I just pull on the
whole mess until it comes free. I manage to get
the front door open and I throw it out into the
street.

This has to stop.

I sit for a moment and finish my warm beer.
Then I put on my coat, light up a cigarette,
and go back out to the street.

Titan leads the rider outside and asks where he is headed.

-I am just heading down the road I guess…

The rider seems unwilling to offer more and Titan does not seem to be bothered by this. The men walk up to the younger rider's bike and stop to look at the vehicle. After a moment Titan snorts,

-Is *that* what you're riding on?

Yes is all that comes from the rider's mouth. His words are in his pockets with his hands.

After a pause, Titan says quietly,

-Holy shit, kid, that is some old bike. What year?

-Seventy-eight.

They stare for moment longer at the old green Kawasaki. It has simple profile lines, and in spite of the road mud speckling the undercarriage, the little bike is clean and rust free.

The young man explains that he's been driving all day through the rain, and Titan, who has many sons, takes it all in silently, pulling on his cigarette all the while. The rider finishes with a resigned sigh and asks where there is a campground near by, but is brusquely cut off by Titan.

-Well, brother, from one rider to the next, we'll find you some dinner and you can make yourself at home in this here garage.

Titan heaves the big garage door open to reveal a warm, well-used room full of big couches, a pool table, and beat-up sound system with huge speakers hung on the walls, a long greasy work bench, and his ride, polished and proud in the middle of the garage.

-This is where the local brotherhood has been

meeting, Titan explains. See, I belong to a riding fellowship, folks from towns and farms around here.

Titan leans his weight back onto his heels and looks around the room proudly before continuing.

-See, an oldie named Sawhorse used to be the leader of our brotherhood. We used to meet at his place.

-Why don't you still meet with him? Tom asks. After a moment Titan responds with the coolness of a gun barrel.

-Well, Sawhorse and his wife died on the road this summer.

Footsteps sound behind them and they turn to see Old Lady approaching with a cup of coffee.

-So is he stayin', Old Man? She hands the stranger the warm cup and gives him an open wink.

-Yeah? Titan laughs a big laugh and the young man smiles too, thinking of nothing better to say or do.

-This boy is welcome here. You did right bringin' him home, Old Lady.

Tom attempts a thank you and is quickly hushed, so he turns instead to his cup of dark coffee. It would give an ear to his gratitude.

The flashing streetlight is the only movement on the street. The snow has stopped falling. The air is still. I turn the corner and begin walking again under the train platform. It is getting late, almost three, and the chances of finding what I am looking for in this cold are slim. But what am I looking for? Perhaps the cold? The exposure. I want to take my clothes off and lie on the ground. It wouldn't take long. I would close my eyes, and in the morning the children from the school across the street would run in a circle around my body, laughing and dancing.

I look up and see an older woman walking down the sidewalk a ways ahead of me. From my first glance I can see she is not a hooker. Or at least not a career woman. But what other reason does she have to be out here in this cold, at this hour? Her shoulders are tense and desperate and she looks straight ahead as she walks.

My heart begins to race again and I keep walking with my head locked forward, as if I don't see her, but my eyes turn subtly in my head. It is very cold and I can see her shivering under her pale blue puffy coat.

We walk right past each other, and keep walking. Maybe I was wrong? Maybe I am an unusual character to her, not what she was expecting to find on the streets of Brooklyn in the middle of the night? My instincts tell me to stop. So I stop. I turn around and look at her as she walks away from me. Walking on the ice I know she has heard me, but she keeps walking. I can see the fear rising from her blue coat like steam. She gets to the corner and she comes to a skipping halt. She stands there for a moment. Still. The streetlights are flashing over her shoulder.

She turns her head and looks back at me. She is half a block away now, but I can see her

eyes. They are clear and purposeful. They are
not inviting or amused. They are resigned.

I turn toward her and I start walking. She
waits for me to catch up with her and, saying
nothing, she starts walking next to me. We
shuffle down the block in silence, turn the
corner, step over my discarded computer, and
enter my apartment.

Inside, little is said.

-Twenty bucks, She says. A statement.

-Sure. A blow job is fine.

-I have to feed my kids.

-OK.

My stomach knots as I slip my pants down and
lie back on my bed. There is a furrow in her
brow. I think it may be better if I turn the
lights off, but there are only the Christmas
lights. I have money in my pants pockets and
I want to watch. I want to watch. She starts
sucking me off, and I find my mind wandering to
her kids. I believe her. I don't care. She is
obviously hard up because clearly she doesn't
do this often. Maybe she did when she was
younger. I don't know.

It goes on and I can she is growing
impatient. She stops for a moment. Her mouth
pulls away from me and her eyes look to the
floor.

-Are you gonna cum?

-I think I need to fuck you, I say. I'm
pretty drunk. I'll give you another twenty.

She mumbles something again about feeding her
kids. She takes her pants down to her ankles
and leans over the side of the bed. I stand
behind her, put a condom on and lean into her.
She has big tits, so I slip my hands under her
blue puffy coat and the sweatshirt and grab

43

hold of them. I start thrusting hard and fast.
She puts her head down, into the bed.

At first she is dry. As I continue, she begins
to breathe heavily. She grows warm and moist.
I build momentum. Her big breasts are spilling
out of my hands.

-Fuck me. She says. I say nothing. I
concentrate on finishing.

-Fuck me. Come on. Come on. That's right.
Come on.

My balls start to tighten up and I am
breathing heavily now. A pain builds from deep
in my ass and rises through me until the knot
in my stomach dissolves into something like
battery acid. I can feel it splashing around,
burning my organs. I cum hard, like passing a
stone.

I pull out and sit on the bed next to her. My
dick is still hard and my balls are tight and
throbbing. She quickly pulls her pants up.

-I can't stay, she says, zipping her puffy
coat back up. The coat seems like it weighs a
lot.

-I have coffee, I offer.

-I have to go. I have to go.

I take another twenty out of my pants and
hand it to her. When she takes the bill, our
hands brush against each other and I notice
how soft her hands are. Hands like a mother's
hands.

She takes a moment to gather herself and then
heads for the door. I don't see her out. She is
gone before I can move, but I hear her say to
no one,

-I have to feed my kids.

The door is closed and I am left there
looking like Porky Pig with my shirt on and

no pants. It is past 4:00 a.m. now. The white walls of my room seem ominous. I look around at the bits and pieces of my life placed purposefully on my shelves and tables: a lock of hair, left from cutting my friend Valerie's hair when she decided to move away from her totalitarian mother; a small plastic frog a patron gave me when I was a dishwasher at the Dundee Dinner Theatre in Omaha; a picture of my grandmother when she was a child of eleven in Iowa. She is sitting on the ground in front of a farmhouse with her legs outstretched toward the camera. On the bottom of her shoes, written onto the photograph, are the words *lefty* and *righty*. There is also a silver ring, inlaid with turquoise stones, hanging from a cord on my desk lamp. It was my father's wedding ring. Above the bathroom, where my mirror used to hang, is a rough cross-stitch on burlap of a sun and moon meeting in a circle. My mother gave it to me the last time I visited her in the hospital.

I slip my pants back on. Then my jacket. I light a cigarette. I peer into my insides. I listen to my chest, my heart. I listen for thoughts to come to me from the hollow of my mind. I look down at my hands to see if they are trembling, and they are still. There is nothing. I am empty.

I take a drag from my cigarette, open the door to the street, and go back out into the night.

How had he found himself here? The question lingered in the rider's mind.

He is heading east toward nowhere. He is in the sanctuary of strangers. It seems that life has always handed him solutions, one after the other, each in their own turn. He tries not to think about where he is coming from or what he is running from. Demons are chasing him across this peaceful countryside. He shakes this thought out of his mind. A respite has been granted. He has found another oasis.

How far did I travel today? On the highway the question seems too literal. A few hundred miles. How far *had* he traveled, though? He still doesn't know where he is going, or what he will find. There is no turning back. That is certain. There is nothing but dust behind him now. His life before this moment seemed clouded and unreal. There is only one choice: forward. Down the road

In the morning he'll go farther. Traveling east through the Midwestern chill. In early spring, the sky quickly jumps from sun to rain. He is riding on a foreign wind, floating unfettered, like a cottonseed.

A side door swings open and Titan rolls in with two beers, his face painted with a shit-eatin' grin. He hands one over and sits down on a milk crate next to the couch. They say nothing, just drink and look out over the bikes. The garage lends itself to easygoing and comfortable silences. A few crickets crawl about the room, singing in response to the chorus of their brethren in the surrounding fields.

When Titan speaks, it is with a gusty sigh.

-You've got me thinking of old Sawhorse. He was the leader of our brotherhood. Well, he was my friend. I've known him for a long time, since about your age I guess. We were just a couple of hell-raising kids. He's dead though, dead and gone.

There is another moment of cricket-filled quiet. Until Titan's need to share his loss brings out a hushed telling of his friend's demise.

-He died on the road for sure. He and his old lady both. We were out on a run, about forty of us. It was a rally for this kid who'd been hit by a car out on ol' Fifty-One. Jimmy Boothe. Jimmy got hit by a car and was laid up in the hospital, no money, his mom a drunk. Jimmy was a good smart boy, though. Anyway the brothers rallied to make money for him to have one of those electronic wheelchairs, poor kid.

Well, we were all out on the highway tearing home rowdy as hell. Sawhorse and his old lady were at the rear of the pack when we rolled up to our exit. Trouble was, a lot of us got up in front of a semi truck. Eighteen-wheeler. A lot of the riders, myself included, blasted out in front and caught the exit.

Sawhorse had been riding his whole life, and he always rode safe. Especially with his baby on back...

This trucker must've gotten nervous with all forty of us swarming around 'im, so he started laying heavy on his brakes just as he was passing that off-ramp.

Sawhorse knew he wasn't gonna get around him and was going too fast to brake like that trucker. The horse was damn close to smacking right up into that truck's rear. So he passed him on the right.

Titan sighed and looked about his old garage. He pulled a cigarette out of his shorts pocket, lit it up and went on.

-Wouldn't ya know there was a goddamn Jeep just...dead, on the shoulder, right off the side

47

of the road.

—Old Horse was gone in a second. Shit.

They sit in silence for a moment before Titan speaks again.

—Listen kid, I don't know why I said all that, with you on the road and all. I sure don't mean to spook ya. I just saw you come in all beat and tired, like Sawhorse and I've been so much before.

Titan sticks a porky finger at the kid's shoes.

—It ain't safe to ride with them sneakers on, boy. The Horse's old lady was wearing sneakers like that when they went down. I guess she put her legs down, before they hit, but I'll never forget her feet... They were all torn up. Mostly they were gone.

The young rider looks down at his old shoes. His mouth is dry from Titan's telling.

—What size shoes you got on, kid?

—Well, the rider says witlessly, nine I guess.

—All right, Titan says to nobody as he gets up. Hope you're comfortable here, boy. We've sure had some good times here.

With that the big man slowly rolls out of the garage, leaving the boy to sleep in the harmonious lull of country cricket hymns.

My first steps are unsure. I am dizzy and my
vision is blurred. The air has dried out
my eyes and a chalky fog has settled over
them. I take a few more steps. I am shaking
uncontrollably. The beer has thinned my blood
and the wind has cut my jacket to ribbons. I
take a few more steps forward and then stop. I
am standing, I realize, in the middle of the
crosswalk. A red hand is flashing in front of
me. Don't walk. Don't walk. Don't walk.

This is very funny to me and I say it aloud.

-Don't walk.

I stand there long enough for the white man
to appear on the sign ahead of me. Walk. This
is so funny. I stand there shaking, a mobile
statuary. Frozen and jolly.

-This is so funny.

I am standing there laughing with my teeth
clicking together and I hear the *bwooap* of
a police cruiser and the cherries of police
lights begin to dance across the steel columns
holding up the train tracks. The car rolls up
from behind and stops alongside of me. I don't
move, and I don't stop laughing. Things have
gotten funnier.

The window rolls down and an officer looks
out at me. I turn my head to look at him, still
shaking and smiling. He is smiling too.

-Evening, of-ficer, I say.

-You got somewhere to be kid?

I think that there has to be some point when
these guys stop calling me kid.

-Well, no s-sir.

He leans back into the cruiser and says
something to his partner. Then he pokes his
head out the window, with an even bigger smile.
I smile back.

-Can I see some identification?

-No sir. S-sorry sir. I don't have it. I wouldn't walk out here alone with my wallet. That's just crazy.

Suddenly he doesn't seem amused, which is strange to me because I thought what I just said was a pretty funny. Perhaps he has no appreciation for irony.

-All right, he says. Why don't you just get in the backseat.

And with this I hear the door locks pop up. The sound makes me think of champagne corks, from work, and I imagine a room full of people cheering. I half raise my arms and attempt a gracious bow, but instead I just teeter to my left and make a half-frozen stumble toward the car.

-All right, kid. The officer grunts and opens the door. As he steps out onto the crosswalk a shrill voice sounds from behind us.

-Heeyehh!

A familiar black woman wearing tight sweatpants and a very tattered gray sweater comes sashaying up to us. She is oblivious to the cold and she speaks loudly with a garrulous smile.

-Hey officer! How are you? Uh-huh. Yeah. What you doing messing with this poor white kid?

The officer tries to speak, but she railroads over him.

-Listen, you just get your butt back in that car and let me handle this one. I mean. It's almost Christmas! *Can a girl work?*

Without waiting for an answer, she hooks my arm and strides purposely toward my apartment. We round the corner and she pulls me down to the entryway. My foot snags on my discarded computer power cable, and I almost fall, but she is strong and steadies me so I can get out my keys. At the lock my hands are bouncing like a hummingbird and I manage to say,

-That was awesome.

-Oh *please*, baby, she says with a wave, which arcs from her knee to above her head. That's just Michael. We went to fuckin' high school together. He's an asshole.

The key finds the lock and the door swings open.

-I like the lights, she says, and pulls me into the apartment.

Inside.

-So. Are you gonna let me fuck you? You are such a pretty little bitch. And you know this pussy is unbelievable.

-I know, I know, I say. Let me think about it.

She is finishing my last beer. It is funny she just helped herself to it. I don't mind, though; I am already pretty drunk, and I am attempting to keep a level head.

-You know, I have this friend who wants me to go to this party on Friday. Just gonna be me and her, and all these drugs, and some guys, you know. You should come.

-Yeah, I say. Maybe.

-Oh, come on, she says. I can tell you're a freak. You'll love it.

I laugh at this, because she is probably right. I could go, and just get fucked up, and be there, and just let whatever happens happen. I'm sure it would be a charming evening. I am sure I'd have a nice time.

She leans over on the bed and grabs a pen from the desk. There is nothing to write on within reach, so she opens *Exile and the Kingdom*, which is lying there, and writes a phone number on the inside cover.

-Just call me.

-OK, I say. Maybe. Maybe.

-Whatever, she says. You're a pussy.

She is laughing and finishes the beer. She slides down off the bed, onto her knees on the floor next to me.

-Come on, she says. I want that cock of yours.

A bit unsteadily, I stand and slip my pants

down. My penis is flaccid, and the smell of pussy and perfume and cum drifts into my nostrils.

-I don't know if I have much left in me.

She smiles at the smell. And puts her hands underneath my balls. She rubs them gently knowing they are sore and with an outstretched tongue begins to lick the end of my cock. She is looking up at me. There is a glint in her eyes, and the corners of her mouth are turned up. I put both of my hands on her shoulders and lean on her. I watch as my dick gets hard and she begins to take the whole thing in her mouth. She works up and down on it, without hurry, looking at me all the while.

-I don't think I can cum. I have had a lot to drink, and...

She says nothing, just works faster, up and down, beginning to moan, and rolling her eyes into the back of her head. I sigh and look up out the window. The sky is slowly changing to blue. There is a line of silver atop all the snow in my backyard. The trees glisten in the stillness outside and a snowbird has begun to call out for his mate.

My dick hits the back of her throat and she lets out a garbled laugh. I look down at her, and she is staring at me again. The glint behind her eyes has become fiery. She slowly pulls her mouth from me and smiles. She takes my hands from her shoulders and moves them to the sides her head.

-Come on, she says, fuck my face.

She opens her mouth and places her lips on the top of my penis. I slide into her and she closes her eyes. I stand there, pushing hard, holding her head. I hit the back of her throat and she begins to moan again. I push harder, stabbing the back of her mouth, again, and again. My elbows start to tremble as my body tightens completely. I thrust and thrust, but there is nothing. I thrust and look down at her. I see her there. She is kind. She is kind.

I stop, and pull away, and fall back on the bed.

-I am sorry. I can't, I just had too much.

She smiles and runs her sweatered arms across her mouth.

-It's OK, honey. You're not hurting *my* feelings.

She stands up and grabs her bag. She leans over on her hip and looks around the apartment, giving me a moment to pull up my pants. I pull a twenty out of my pocket, which is gone and in her bag before it can even register that an exchange has been made.

-All right, honey! I gotta split!

I can't help but smile. I don't know how she does it. I walk her to the door and open it for her. The street is pale gray, lit by the dawn. All the second-story windows reflect the blazing sun.

She strides out into the avenue, breathing in the morning. She swings her arms in time with her steps, and I hear her voice lift up into song:

Ding dong the ho is dead

The nasty ho

The dirty ho

Ding dong the dirty ho is dead

Ding dong the bitch got killed

Sucking dick

Eatin' it

Ding dong the dumb-ass bitch

got shot right in the head!

And then she is gone. Her voice trails away around the corner and down the street. I close the door. I stand in the middle of the room. I don't know what to do. I want to call someone, but what would I say? I am not really tired and I don't want to lie on my bed. So I just lie there, on the floor, with no blanket or pillow.

I'm not sure what I have to do tomorrow. Rather, I know that there's nothing to do. I want to go outside and sit out on my Brooklyn rooftop, read something, and eat an orange. Small things really make life come together for me. Oatmeal cookies. A can of Coca-Cola. Little moments of unarguable perfection.

Sun creeps in through the dusty windows of the old garage, which is dull and quiet in the morning light. The man stretches his legs out over the side of the couch. He gathers up his few possessions and slings his bag over his shoulder. He takes a few steps toward his quiet motorcycle and slides his hand over the faded green tank. He speaks unselfconsciously to his bike.

—Are you ready, old bud? It's just you and me.

Opening up the garage door, he pushes the bike out into the driveway. The kids are already up and about. They're running across the yard, rushing through chores they've done a hundred times before.

Soft light sifts obliquely through the trees above him and the rider looks out over the open fields surrounding the farmhouse. A couple of horses toss around in the back. Rows of cabbage and green beans seem to stretch on forever.

—Good morning, mister! It's Fart.

—Well, good morning, Fart, the rider replies, not bothering to hide his smile.

—Are you going to drive away today, mister? Fart squawks.

—Yeah, I sure am Fart. I'm getting back on the road, to see where it'll take me.

—Well, Fart says with a laugh as he runs off into the yard, watch out for the sky fallin' on yer head, mister! Ha ha!

With that, the fat boy is back to work, barking orders and running the other young ones through their chores in the yard.

The rider starts his bike up, and lets it run to warm up the engine. He reaches up to the big oak leaves hanging above the drive and stretches his own body with a yawn. Behind him there is the bang of a screen door and from the house a jolly Titan cries out,

- All right all right, don't you be taking off without a proper good-bye.

Old Lady follows behind Titan, barefoot, holding her boots in her hand.

-Here, honey, you can't be riding around in those sneakers, offers Old Lady, handing her boots over to the boy.

After a shocked pause, the young rider quickly responds, -I can't take your boots, ma'am.

-Don't call me ma'am, snaps Old Lady. These are just as old as hell. Just try them on. The young man doesn't move, so Titan encourages him further, saying,

-Listen kid, I bought her new boots for Christmas. This is just hand-me-downs. Go ahead and try them on.

Thinking of his soaked feet the day before, the young rider swallows down something like pride and pulls off his worn sneakers. Old Lady's boots slip on snuggly but comfortably. To this she laughs,

-My Old Man always said I had feet like a fella.

The rider lifts his knees and presses his feet into the ground, marching in place.

-They fit all right. They fit good.

He bends and picks up his old sneakers and says,

-Could I trade you for these? I can't bring them and maybe one of the kids would like them.

-That sounds fair, Titan says with a nod as he takes up the young man's shoes. It's a trade, then.

With that the rider swings his leg over his bike and says,

-Thank you, Titan. Thank you, Old Lady.

-Ride safe, brother, Titan says, his huge voice almost trembling. He extends his free hand to the young man. I wish I were going out on the road with ya.

They exchange a warm grasp and say no more. Old Lady turns to shoo the kids back into the yard as the rider shifts the bike into gear. Rested, renewed, and filled with a feeling akin to hope, he pulls smoothly out of the driveway and turns onto the highway. The sun is rising on the horizon ahead and the road lays out languidly before him.

In the morning I am vanished. Waking comes like a ripe peach splitting down the sides. I gasp and come slightly off the floor, reaching out in confusion. I move toward the afternoon sunlight pouring in through the windows. The light cuts across my face and arms in oblique rays that dry my skin. I settle back into the carpet and lie still again.

There are no witnesses—just me, alone on the floor. The future is rolling forward, looking deader than ever. A childhood memory is playing through my head like an eight-millimeter film being projected inward. The memory starts with rain on the windows of a grade school classroom. It was the last day of school. In the afternoon the spring rain turned fierce and sirens filled the neighborhoods with ominous wails. Next I remember huddling in the gym with all the students in my class, wild with anticipation, as the tornado sirens continued to blare from the distance.

The storm passed uneventfully and we were released out into a rain-soaked neighborhood and a summer of freedom. As I walked home the sky was beautiful. The streets were slick, still saturated, and I jumped into a huge puddle. The inviting pool was no puddle. There was a gaping hole in the street, filled with water, some unfinished work, some task left undone. I pounced into this still, reflective pool triumphantly to find myself submerged, over my head in muddy liquid. I thought I'd jumped through a wormhole. I thought I'd already reached the end of my short life. When I resurfaced, I scrambled out onto the street and shook myself ineffectually. I was still on the way home, soaked like a newborn child on the way to live. The Midwestern sky was brilliant, almost cobalt. I delighted in my soggy shoes and my chafing thighs, my clothes fused to my

skin. I ran home joyous. I ran to tell the
world of my discovery. Of my success. Of my
survival.

Blanket snow troubles hedgerows with overmuch weight. Frosted window. White aluminum muntins holding frozen panes that emanate visible cold into the room.

A fan switches on, moving air through the vents. Hysteria, dementia, unrestrained grief, irrational fear, animal lust, restless articulation, and induced submission are mixed and circulated through the corridors and vestibules, spreading the photons, negative ions, and the stink of insanity. The mixture is palpable and the room is uncanny. The white sheets have sharp edges that can cut or maim. The fluorescent light, pouring from above, filtered by a corrugated plastic sheet, has visible holes in it, through which anything could pass.

All one must do is look into the light. Reach out with the mind. And come face to face with an inhuman obscenity. Lovemaking might occur. Or murder.

A single blink, from an eye that sits in a face, which lies atop a skull and makes up a girl's head, which could be called nothing other than wrecked beauty. Strapped. Restrained.

In the darkness of a single blink…

The room shudders in cataclysm. Portals open and close. Flights of angels are slain and are falling from an unknowable sky. An Antichrist is born, and fourteen numerologists, each sitting or standing, all of them writing with the nubs of pencils, are struck dumb nine seconds away from prophesying the moment of the child's birth. The seed of a Joshua tree germinates in a desert on the other side of the earth. It will grow and offer a little shade to a prophet who will sing a last song to a sleeping lover before walking out of the desert to be killed in a televised execution.

And so on... Nothing stops happening. It just stops being perceived by the wrecked beauty as eyes flicker open.

The room resettles in whiteness. Glancing out a fogged window to twisted, snow-laden hedgerows. The fight against tranquilizers and psychotropics continues until spring.

PINIONED BY LIGHT

It's Christmas. Lights hang over the streets,
suspended between buildings in Brooklyn. Night
has fallen early, and Grand Avenue is bustling
with families and revelers, shuffling to and
from warmth. A light snow covers the street
lamps and the mailboxes. The streets are slick,
edged with frosty curbs. Everyone is bundled
for the cold. Rose-colored cheeks splash the
white and gray night with jovial radiance. On
another day that same old Dominican man would
be drawn back into his stoop, shoulders curled
over his stomach and his eyes wandering vaguely
over the passersby. Tonight he stands with a
half-open smile. He looks at me as I walk by.
He acknowledges me. He nods his head and his
smile grows wider. I smile back.

The windows of the row houses are all glowing
with bright eyes set into their vinyl-sided
faces. The houses look down at me as I pass,
and they smile at me. I smile back.

Between Leonard Street and Manhattan Avenue,
I stop and slip down three steps to stand
before Frank's place. Frank. As usual, his
house is the most boisterous on the street.
There are Christmas lights around the window
shaped like little Texas flags. I think of
Christ in the manger being approached by three
crazy old oilmen who followed an angel shaped
like a lone star all through the night. Perhaps
the next messiah will be born a Texan. Maybe
it's Frank.

My finger hangs on the buzzer and I am greeted
by a burst of laughter and loud voices and
Frank standing in the doorway.

-Merry Christmas! he says, his voice shaking
with enthusiasm.

-Merry Christmas, Frank, I say.

He reaches out and pulls me into a bear
hug. He is the first person who has touched
me in three days. His hug is so familiar. I
put my arms around him and put my head on his
shoulder. I don't let go, but I don't return
his squeeze, and he knows something is wrong.
Without needing to ask why, or what, he pulls
me into in his apartment

-Come in Thomas! Let's get you a drink.

The room is full of familiar faces. A drink is pushed into my hand and Frank leads me around the room, nodding hello and smiling. Everyone is laughing and talking at once. These are the Christmas stragglers of New York City. People whose families live somewhere else and who are trapped in a half-empty city, which still shakes with the honesty of ethnic celebration. It is Frank's job to give these orphan-for-a-day folks a home for the night.

Frank and I don't speak directly as we move through the crowded room. When he feels I have built up enough momentum, he breaks off from me. He has left me in front of a face, framed in long chestnut hair, whose name I can't remember. She is dressed up like a candy cane: a red chiffon dress, with white lace. It is low cut, and her white stockings have the silhouette of a Playboy bunny cut out of them. She is the Christmas tree that everyone crowds around, hoping to be handed presents.

-I luv New York in Christmas. Don't you? And I can't believe that it snowed. I luv snow so much.

-Yeah, I say, the snow was good, but it has gotten pretty black and greasy.

She sort of laughs, and says,

-Oh, it doesn't last long. But it is so beautiful when it is falling. I luuvvv it. I luuvvv New York in Christmas.

-Yeah, I say, it's pretty. The city feels so empty.

-It makes me so lonely, she pouts, Frank said I could crash here with everyone if I wanted to, but there isn't a lot of space. I don't want to spoon on the futon with his drunk brother. Everyone would probably sleep through him raping me.

I laugh at this. This is the first time I

65

have laughed today. In a few days, I realize.
The laughter comes from my tight chest and the
warmth is unfamiliar. The laughter stops in
my throat. And my head drops a little bit. I
realize I don't want to be here. I look over
my shoulder and Frank is looking at me while
holding a conversation with someone. His eyes
are sparkling and thrilled. They say, *This girl
is a sure thing, Thomas*. He is probably talking
about North Korea, and nukes, and America's
nonproliferation mistakes, and bald eagles, and
pancakes.

-I am gonna have a cigarette.

I say it before I look at her and when I turn
my head back, her eyes are soft and imploring.
She is holding her drink just away from her
lips.

-Oh, she says moving closer to me, can I have
one?

-Of course, I say, as I shoulder through the
crowd toward the door.

Frank grabs my arms as I walk past him. He
smiles at me and I warmly smile back.

-I love you, buddy, he says.

-I know, man. I know. Thanks.

I push through the door and start walking up
the steps, going home.

-Hey! Where are you going? She sounds really
concerned, like something very serious just
happened.

-Oh, you know.

My voice is wavering, but I continue,

-I thought I'd go home and walk around a
little bit.

-Can I come? She is hopeful.

-No. No, I don't think so, I say dryly.

66

-Well, where are you going? She is growing annoyed.

-Oh, I say, putting as much cheer in my voice as I can muster, I am gonna go home and fuck a hooker.

The ruckus from the house is suddenly muffled quiet, and we are standing there on the steps in a silent glass case, as if we were underwater, or maybe trapped in a snow globe.

-And if I can't find I hooker, I am gonna track down that old tranny on Knickerbocker and see if she'll fuck me in the ass. It is Christmas, you know. Maybe she'll be into it.

My candy-cane friend stands there with her jaw open, a stunned look in her eyes. She is painted with disbelief. I am not sure if it's because she thinks I might actually go fuck a hooker or because I am turning down a chance to sleep with her. Probably both.

The volume to the house is suddenly turned back on. There are cars driving by and people laughing on the streets. Inside Frank's house there is controlled insanity and chili cheese dip.

He got that recipe from me.

It hurts to laugh, but I laugh and walk down the street, not turning to look back. I walk toward the river. I don't want to go home. I don't want anything. I am just enjoying the fact that my laughter is painful.

A brisk crosswind cuts its way across the road.
Spring has not yet settled in, and riding in
the morning and at night invites the chill to
slip its fingers under your skin. Still euphoric
about last night's solace, the rider smiles
inside his helmet. The cold is no bother.
The sun crawls its way upward and bathes the
countryside in light. He is gracefully sailing
his motorcycle through Elysian Fields.

Crops have not taken in the fields yet this
early in Spring, but he imagines...

He imagines rows of wheat turning into low
huddled patches of spinach and cabbage. The
air has changed its hue, from the reflection
of heavenly golds to a verdant green, wet
with saturation. There is a field break a
couple of miles ahead. Rows of trees stretch
perpendicularly to the road marking the
meandering trail of a river.

The bike is humming and the rider is
relaxed. The hypnotizing road has suspended
his thoughts. There is no sign of rain, and as
the tree line slowly grows in size, a sense of
expectation begins to fill in his quiet chest.

Through the trees an old steel suspension
bridge begins to show its crown. There are no
cars on the highway and the sense of excitement
begins to make the rider tremble. He rolls the
throttle back and opens up the engine. The bike
is old, so it is slow gaining speed in the
upper gears. The wind picks up, and the trees
and the bridge begin to swell. The crosswind
buffets the rider, and in response he lies down
over the tank with his eyes just peaking over
the handlebars.

The air slides over his back and he slips
down the highway like an eel. He glances down
at the speedometer and the needle is pushing
a hundred and still bobbing forward. The bike
somehow grows silent as the engine noise

struggles to keep up with the speed. The air courses over him. The trees rapidly approach and his focus narrows unflinchingly ahead. The crosswind is the only witness and pushes disapprovingly on the bike. But the machine and the man are in communion and want nothing more than to break through the wall of physics and reality. The bridge will disappear and the river will open up beneath them. The tires will cling to the air and they will float across the water like a crane. He will dip his bill into the surface of the water to pluck out a wriggling fish.

Suddenly, bike and rider are overwhelmed by green as they break the tree line and the air cools dramatically. The canopy of the trees blocks out the sun momentarily as rider and bike burst onto the old steel bridge. The bridge emanates an icy aura, which has accumulated from years of soaking in damp river air. They throttle out over the expanse, the girders flashing by in a blinding strobe. The rider's eyes are frozen ahead of him. They are moving well over a hundred miles and hour, eight thousand revolutions per minute. The flashing pylons of the open bridge are close enough to stick out a leg and touch.

He drops the throttle suddenly, pulls the clutch in and grabs a handful of brake. The front of the bike dips so fast that he has to hug the tank with his legs or be thrown over the handlebars. He presses down his right foot and engages the rear brake, which locks up immediately. He can release his foot and the brake, but instead he pushes harder. The rear tire begins to screech and smoke and the bike fishtails out to the right, dangerously close to the side rails.

-Ride it out, he says inside his helmet, as he grits his teeth and hangs on.

The bike could flip or hit the rail. He could
be thrown up into the steel rafters or be
tossed out into the river. Instead, the bike is
still and innocently idling in the middle of
the empty bridge. He is calm, his pulse keeping
time with the ticking engine. He pulls the
bike straight and off to the right of the lane,
against the side rail.

He kills the engine and dismounts. He looks
down the highway to see emptiness in both
directions. Only two or three cars have passed
him all morning. Stepping to the side rail, he
puts a foot up on a steel curb and leans on his
elbow over the open ledge. The wind buffets him
as it races down the trail of the river.

He hoists himself up and hangs his top
half over the bridge and takes the wide river
in. The banks are black, fecund. He smiles,
watching the muddy beaches overtaken endlessly
by the conspiratorial waves. A curving alluvial
ridge wages a pitched battle, twisting to and
fro against the incessant current.

Suddenly there is a roar behind him and he
turns, startled, to see a semi truck bearing
down on him. The bridge is divided into two
single lanes and he and his bike are hiked up
against the rail with inches between them and
the road. Whether the trucker sees him or not,
the truck doesn't slow. The eighteen-wheeler
tears past him with the sound of an avalanche.
He is pressed between the wind of the river
and the explosion of displaced air from the
truck. He is held, suspended there, his heart
weightless in his chest.

Then the truck is through and junking over
the bridge and down the road and off to god
knows where.

-Sweet shit. That was close, the rider says
breathlessly.

He looks down the road and sees another

70

truck in the distance, shooting the same piece of road he had just raced across. He hops back on his bike, fires up the engine and continues on. He leaves the bridge and the water and the moment behind.

A long concrete retaining wall separates
me from the river. The waterfront has been
renovated and rebuilt with a high-design
boardwalk that melds and curves along the
path of the water. Rusted machinery remains,
thrusting out from the water. Developers have
rebuilt a shiny reflection of the decrepit
machines in polished concrete and brushed
steel. The vibrations of this once busy port
have been all but stilled with layers of
asphalt and pressure-treated wood planking.

I am staring over the wall, looking at the
remnants of an old dock still clinging to the
shore. Every day, more of it is washed away.
All that is left is a few rotted posts and
sickly looking boards.

There is no one around, so I hop the wall
down to the old shore. I am surprised when
my feet hit sand. The feeling of tiny rocks,
unattached by mortar, still organic in their
chaotic individuality, has become unfamiliar. I
have the impulse to take off my shoes and bury
my feet in the sand. It is too cold, though,
and my toes would freeze. The wind is strongest
here at the water's edge. It whips a chill
off the surface of the water that slips right
through my clothes and into my skin, massaging
my bones. I feel like a naked, bone-white
skeleton, dancing unseen under the light of the
moon.

Opening my mouth, I suck in a mouthful of
the river air, and I can feel the chill on
the front of my spine. I stick my tongue out
and raise my arms like a seagull. With a few
skips and a hop, I spring out onto one of the
posts rising out of the water. Ice has formed
along its greasy sides and I have to let my
body relax to keep my balance on the slippery
pedestal.

My shoulders go slack and my stomach drops.
The cold is suddenly very soothing and I

raise my gaze to look out across the river to the city on the other side. Manhattan is pandemonium crowned by an indifferent sky. The water, as well, shrugs its way downstream, past the carnival, on its way to the ocean.

The wooden post I am standing on is probably more than a hundred years older than I am. When it was first hammered into the surface of the river bottom, this piece of sandy beach was surrounded by a different landscape altogether. Cargo ships carrying whale meat and oil, immigrants and slaves.

This dock shuddered under millions of footsteps. It was deafened by shouts in dozens of languages. It was the gateway to possibility, hope, exploit, and disappointment. And now, like a lighting rod, I stand delirious atop it, witnessing the greatest collision of mankind and nature that has ever unfurled itself across the surface of the earth, New York City.

I cannot tell the end from the beginning. The moment is so huge, it suffocates time and pours into me. It fills me. It excavates me. My hands are outstretched and my eyes are open, but I do not know what I see. I can only feel the tremendous sigh of being there among all that has passed by before and all that is sure to follow.

The noise of a siren floats across the water. An ambulance is racing up the highway. I can see its tiny flashing light ducking in between cars. The highway is gridlocked up ahead and I watch it come to a halt. The lights atop the ambulance seem to spin faster in the face of futility. The howl of the siren could be the agonizing voice of a young mother keening for her dying son.

I am afraid someone is dying inside the back of the ambulance: a teenage immigrant whose lifeblood incessantly spills out of him while a brusque woman from Queens dressed in an EMS jacket holds his hand.

The cars don't move, so I jump back onto the shore, sure I am witnessing someone die because they are stuck in traffic.

Suddenly I am cold, unbearably cold. I gather my arms around my chest and squeeze myself for warmth. I begin the long walk home.

Farther down the road, he pulls off to the shoulder. The afternoon has grown late and the high sun is pounding down. There is no fuel gauge on the gas tank. He guesses there is about twenty miles left in the tank. There hasn't been a sign of a town in almost an hour.

There is less traffic out on these old highways. The gas stations and towns have been passed over by the big, corporate travel plazas on faster interstates. He has always avoided huge interstate highways. Everyone who drives on them seems to be pissed off about something, racing down the road at eighty miles an hour, shivering in their air conditioning. People who live along older highways see fewer travelers and more local folk. So that's how they treat you—like a neighbor.

He sees a gravel utility road ahead so he slows the bike down and turns off the main road. He kills the engine and leans the bike over on its side-stand. Then he takes his helmet off, and wipes the sweat off his head with his gloved hand. He takes his gloves off, which are covered in road grime.

-Where did this heat come from?

Unzipping his bag, he shuffles around for his water bottle. It is empty. He frowns, realizing he didn't think to fill it at Titan's place. He taps the near-empty gas tank and it responds with a hollow thud. His stomach growls a retort, and he reaches into his wallet. He knows there is little money left, but he counts the bills anyway. Thirty-two dollars.

-What a shit-storm, he says aloud.

With a sigh he leans against his bike. For the first time in days the breeze is warm. Leaning against the bike, he looks out over a bare field. The ground has been turned up and left unplanted. Off the road a few yards away there is a long column of wooden telephone

75

poles that line the road. The country has flattened out and the poles seem to stretch out into infinity, getting smaller and smaller down the road.

He looks up and across the wire to see rows and rows of black birds. They are high up and can't be heard from the road, they look like a disembodied crowd waiting in line. He watches them, marveling at how many there are and how still they seem. There must be hundreds of them just basking in the sunlight. They are still.

With a grin he marches off the road, his feet crunching into dark earth. He moves slowly, not wanting to spook the birds. He pokes around on the ground until he finds a sizable clod of dirt. He picks it up and creeps up to the pole. The birds shift uneasily on the wire, but remain fixed on their spot.

He lifts up the clod and with all his might he heaves it onto the cracked wooden pole. The shock races up its length and suddenly the birds alight, one after the other, like a huge string of flying black dominos. They let out a cacophonous roar and the air is suddenly filled with a swarm of desperately flapping wings.

Without waiting for retaliation from the birds, he scrambles back onto his bike. In one movement he is throwing his leg over and sliding his helmet back on. He fires the bike back up and lets the engine roar in harmony with the birds. He yells as well,

-Kaw! Kaw!

Then he tosses the bike into gear and sprints off down the road, laughing under a sky full of circling black birds.

From atop the Pulaski Bridge, the grand facade of Manhattan rises above the water. I have walked a long way from home. My body is feeling stiff and brittle. My neck is craned toward the edge of the footbridge so I can watch the city as I walk. The water flowing through the canal below looks icy and razor-edged, as though filled with thousands of trapped black sharks, their dorsal fins restlessly churning the surface of the river.

My father jumped or fell or was pushed from a bridge. It was documented as a suicide but there was no evidence and no investigation. He was out on the road, far from home and looking for work. It doesn't actually matter to me if it was or wasn't a suicide. I'll never know what really happened anyway. It is a mystery. The speculation haunts me.

I cannot walk atop a precipice without contemplating the leap. Looking down, I imagine my body being torn by sharp waves with rows of merciless teeth. I shudder and turn my head back to the walkway. Ahead, huddled in the corner of a scenic overlook at the center of the bridge, a figure clings to the steel rails and looks down at the bundled pylons rising out of the water below.

The figure is wrapped in layers of coats and hoods, a shapeless form in the night. Something pricks my attention suddenly. I don't know if it is the unforgiving wind, the utter absence of Christmas carols, or the fixity with which the figure stares out over the water wherein I had just considered my absolution, but I change my pace and stop abruptly as I am about to pass the figure. I cough quietly and take my place purposefully alongside the stranger.

I do not try to steal a glance into the shadowed hood. I say nothing. I just stand there in the cold, looking down into the dark water. I am not wearing much, just a red

T-shirt under my leather jacket. I dressed
without thinking about the cold and I envy
the layers of down that envelop the figure. I
notice, though, that despite the layers, this
person is visibly shivering. I am not sure if
the cold is causing such a violent tremble.

Not knowing what to say, I reach into my
pocket for my cigarettes. I push up a filter
and offer it to the figure. The hooded face
turns toward me, revealing the face of a lovely
woman. She has extremely broad check bones,
like Nefertiti or something, with porcelain
white skin. Her cheeks elegantly stained with
tears. She stares at me with unapologetic eyes.
There is no accusation in her gaze, no fear,
only an intense scrutiny. I am transfixed. I see
myself in the reflection of intense pain. And
fear. And accusation.

I open my mouth to speak, but nothing comes
out. She simply outstretches a hand, slender,
like those of a Balinese shadow puppet, and
plucks the cigarette from my pack and says,

-The water looks cold.

She doesn't wipe away her tears or move her
gaze. She just stares at me, waiting.

I try to hand her my lighter, but she does
not take it, so I cup the cigarette in my
hands, close to her face, and strike the wheel.
The flame briefly emblazons her face, giving
contrast to her high cheekbones and sharp jaw.
It only lasts for a second, but I am thinking *I
have never seen a face like that*. Her features
all seem to combat each other. She has dark
almond eyes with thin curved lips, and an
overlarge cleft under her nose.

I light up a cigarette for myself. I look
back out over the water.

-Walk with me to my place, I say, We'll talk.
It's cold.

-Your place, huh? She huffs. After a moment of silence she speaks again over the wind.

-Do you know where a girl can get some mint chocolate chip ice cream?

I laugh aloud. Out there on the bridge, with this strange girl, who I'm half-certain was about to extinguish herself. I laugh again for no reason. Nothing else is said as we walk back to my apartment.

The blue coveralls seem to hold up the old black man who is leaning against the gas pump. His coveralls are stiff and soiled with engine grease and numberless days of sweat. The man's face is contoured with lines carved by the sun. His hands are strong and able. He toys with a shop rag, constantly wringing it tight at his waist.

The engine of the rider's motorcycle clicks thirstily like a horse panting after being ridden until wet. The rider lifts his leg over the bike and stands on the solid ground. His body still seems to vibrate. With so much time on the bike he is beginning to lose his land legs. He thinks he'll take a step, but instead he just sways in the wind. He thinks better of walking just yet and instead pulls his helmet off.

-Evening, son, the old mechanic says.

They stare at each other for a moment without saying anything more. Overhead a full sun looms, gathering warmth. A breeze wicks the sweat off the rider's forehead, leaving a cool itchy sensation.

-You look beat to shit, son, says the mechanic.

-Yeah, I bet I do, sir. Been riding all day. Could you fill it up for me?

The attendant doesn't respond. He just takes a walk around the rider and his bike. He crouches down and looks at the panting engine. Then he stands up again and looks in a similar way at the rider, scrutinizing his face for details.

-I'll be honest, son, I can't say I can tell which o' you looks worse. The bike's in better shape I suppose. Chain could use some lube. You're as pale as a Sunday sheet. How long you been riding?

-I was up with the sun this morning. I stayed
over in Marathon last night with some folks I
met on the road. The rider's words are distant,
coming unattached from him before they leave
his body.

-Marathon, The older man muses, never heard
of it. Must be pretty far off, son. You're
making good time. Where you headed in such a
big hurry you went and missed your lunch?

The rider thinks a moment. He asks himself
where he ate lunch. All he sees is the road
in front of him, mile markers dragging by. He
shakes his head as if coming out of a daze and
says,

-Yeah. Yeah, I musta missed lunch.

The old man in blue coveralls circles around
the bike again and then steps up close to the
rider. He gives him a warm pat on the shoulder.
They are close together, the wind mingling
between him. The old man squints his dark eyes
at the young man. He looks at him as if he is a
boy. He looks at him with all the reproachful
love of a father looking down at his son, who
has let a firecracker off too close to his finger.
He gives the young rider another pat on his
shoulder and says,

-There is a diner there on the corner. I know
it doesn't look like much, but it has got the
best goddamn biscuits and gravy you're ever
gonna eat.

It is not a suggestion, or even a demand.
What the old man says is just so. The young
rider nods his head and starts shuffling in the
direction of the diner. He doesn't give a worry
to his bike, or his things. He doesn't think
about the little bit of money he has left in
his wallet. He passes through the screen door
and is sitting at the counter with his third
empty glass of water and a plate scraped clean
of biscuits and gravy before he realizes where

he is.

He looks out the window to see his bike pulled alongside a gas station across the street. He sees an old black man leaning with ease against the pump. Through the screen door a young woman in jeans with curly auburn hair comes into the diner with a wiry-haired dog at her side. She smiles politely at him as she sits down at the counter with an empty seat in between them. Coming out of a fog, the details are overwhelming. There's a woman behind the counter serving the girl a cup of coffee. The waitress is a hearty matron, wearing an apron that says YOUR FLAPJACKS OR MINE? She holds the pot of coffee up to the young man with a toothy smile and the rider nods. A cup of coffee might wake him up a bit before he gets back on the road.

—Is that your bike out there?

He turns to the sound of the young woman's voice sitting next to him. Again, he is overwhelmed by the details: the loose curls of her hair and the flecked rose of her cheeks, her small breasts beneath a gray sweatshirt and her shapely legs held under tight denim.

—Is that your bike out there? she repeats patiently, drawing his eyes to her own.

He snaps awake suddenly. He grows red, knowing he is stupidly staring at her like a monkey looking at a crowd of people in the zoo.

—Yeah. Yes. I am sorry. I have been on the road a couple days. I am really out of it. This is the first I've eaten today, sorry.

She was scowling at him, but her brow loosens up and her mouth opens into a smile bright enough to melt glaciers.

—Oh sweetie, I'm sorry I spooked ya. So, which way you headed?

She speaks to me of pain. She speaks to me of love. She speaks with unguarded eyes. I watch and listen to her tell the story that in this moment she needs to tell.

-How do we continue to love when we know it will cause us so much pain? I have accumulated so much scar tissue. I have hurt the people that I love most in the world. I was always afraid that I would give my whole soul to someone, create an unbreakable bond with them, a blood knot. This bond would always be there. It will be there with me until death and maybe into the next life. I feel like I am carrying the weight of this. Maybe I've carried it through many lives. It's a curse. Because no matter what I do, I will push that love away and end up alone...in pain. That is my life. I can feel this person out there somewhere but I can't find him.

She stops for a moment and runs her spoon through the milky film left in her ice cream bowl. I realize I am holding my breath. I open my mouth and inhale deeply and it comes out in a hoarse gust.

Her eyes rise from the bowl and spoon to meet my own. She regards me as I stare at her face and blood and warmth begin to rush into my head. I feel lightheaded. She is so beautiful. She is extremely thin, but her arms are muscular and articulate. Her dark brown hair is cut to her shoulders with straight bangs running over thick eyebrows. Dark eyes set into pale skin. She is beautiful.

She holds herself comfortably despite the shabbiness of my apartment. I had insisted we sit on the floor. I have not yet lain on my bed. I've been sleeping on the floor. There is no way, at this juncture, to explain to her why I have forsworn my bed. I don't think about it. She hasn't raised any protest, so I've offered no explanation.

—Do you regret your decisions? she asks.

I don't know what to say to her so I don't say anything, but I feel something very powerful stirring inside me. This moment is shared fragility and makes me feel like silver angel wings will burst from my back and encircle her. The dawn is an hour or so off and my room is heavy around the stillness of her voice.

My back is hunched over and tense. It is unlikely that any angels will find their way into this room, so this instinct to protect her just boils in me and travels up to the furrow in my brow.

—It doesn't matter, she continues. I am a ghost. Haunted. Haunted and alone.

—I believe I have a great capacity for love.

My interruption hangs in the air between us. She smiles at me and I am forced to turn my eyes away from her. I am ashamed.

—I should go, she says. Can I get a cab from here?

—Sure, I say.

Then there is a silence between us. We are both held, as if by an unseen hand.

—Are you…are you OK? I ask quietly, thinking of the bridge I found her on a few hours before.

She smiles and her cheekbones lift close to her eyes.

—Of course, she says in a child voice.

I don't argue. With a nod of resignation I lift myself off the floor of my apartment and I extend a hand to help her up. She takes it and I feel how warm her hand has become. I squeeze it gently as I help her to her feet, and she squeezes mine in return. Blood courses through

84

our hands, through permeable skin, back and forth between our arms.

She stands for a moment with her hand in mine and now I can look at her eyes without flinching. Her mouth opens slightly and air is pulled in sharply over her lips. I start to say something, but words don't come. My throat just sort of gurgles. Our hands come apart and I can feel the moisture cooling on my palm. I look down expecting to see blood on my fingertips, but there's just skin and lifelines.

She begins to slide on her layers of sweater and jacket and coat. Her tiny form is hidden away under wool and Gore-Tex and down. I throw on my leather jacket and she asks,

-Won't you be cold?

-Yes, I say. I like the cold.

-You're full of shit, she says, but I like you.

She chortles a bit, pleased with herself. She just called me out on something, but I don't understand what it is.

-Warm is good too, I say.

I shrug off my jacket and pick up my greatcoat. Now I have woolen armor. I feel less exposed.

-Come on girl, I say, let's get you in a cab.

We walk down the few blocks to Grand Street, where we'll find a cab. Behind us the sun has begun to illuminate the low-hanging clouds, peaking through the buildings. I look up to see a small faded blue balloon caught in the ironwork of a fire escape. It's huddled next to the cold brick face of the building. I wonder how long it has been trapped there. A little hand let it slip from its grasp and watched it float skyward, only to get caught, within eye's view, in the grate of the fire escape. So close, but too far out of reach to ever touch again.

The streets are completely vacant. Not a soul or a storefront flickers with life. Alone in a city of eight million, there is just the two of us. A gust of cold wind whips across the avenue and our bodies come close enough for her puffy coat to brush the sleeve of my wool coat. The contact makes a synthetic scratching sound and I look down to see her bare hands opening and closing into fists. We are leaning on each other slightly. This is as close as we have been to each other the whole night. I want her to burrow through the folds of my coat and into my chest. I want to lead her back to my apartment and lay down with her and close my eyes and sleep. When we wake we would be in another place. We would be other people. We would make love and it would be simple, and beautiful.

-Are you sure you're OK? I ask.

-Yes! Yes, I told you. She snaps this time.

I have annoyed her somehow. Then she turns to me, her head moving with a gust of wind, which whips the tips of her bobbed hair up into the corners of her mouth. Her face softens and she asks quietly,

-What is your name?

I am stunned. I realize we have spent the whole night together talking and I don't know her name. It dawns on me suddenly, how easy it was to be with her. To sit and talk and listen.

-Thom. Thom, I say, with an *h*. My name is Thomas. Thom.

-Hmm, she muses. A Thomas. Well, Thomas, my name is Emile.

-OK, Emile, when are we going to see each other again?

-I don't know. Never. Soon.

And in that moment I love her. It hits me like a semi truck. I don't want her to leave. This tension threatens to pull my body apart. We have reached the inevitable moment. She just looks at me with her open eyes and with the effortlessness of a mother nudging her child to walk, she cuts through the folds of armor encircling my chest. The ghosts swimming around my head are banished with a silent howl. Something wells up from deep within me. A burning, painful and fiery. It is like my hidden self forces its way out of the hot sands in which it was buried.

And without a word more, she lifts one arm toward the street. Her wrist unfurls like a white handkerchief from the window of a departing locomotive, and there on the empty street a lone cab lazily turns a corner and rolls toward us.

It comes to a stop in front of us, impatiently idling. She opens the door and begins to climb in.

I am not sure what to do. I want to cry out. I am shaking. I almost start to get into the cab with her, but she stops and turns toward me. Our eyes search each other.

She suddenly reaches out and takes my head into her hands. I see a kiss full of motion and confusion, and guileless love, but there is no kiss. She softly draws me close to her, nose to nose, and gazing gently into me she says,

-No kissing.

Then the door is closed and the cab is scrambling down the street. Her hand outstretched, fingers curled like Ophelia's bouncing along the riverbed.

He is walking a half step behind her,
conscious of the cool sun bringing red into
her hair and the undulating sway of her boot-
clad swagger. She had introduced herself as
Elise and marched out of the diner, dragging
him behind. Her dog follows them, smiling and
tailless, down the narrow country road.

After only a few yards they have left the
small town behind and the only sound is the
wind and their boot-falls on gravel. He looks
over his shoulder to see the small cluster of
buildings like a circle of wagons around his
motorcycle alone in the center.

—My house is real close, she says, and runs
off ahead.

The dog, whose name is Mickey, dashes in
front of her to retrieve a huge branch from the
yard and drags it to the young woman.

—The dog thinks he's bigger than he is. Her
voice is full of love for the dog. She picks
up the stick and throws it capably across the
yard. Her house is small, and nestled under
trees alongside the country road. The mailbox
is decorated with THE HANSENS in red paint in
what is obviously the handwriting of a small
child.

Elise is standing still in the center of the
yard. The dog continues to jump with gleeful
oblivion.

There is a moment between them. They take
each other in. Reflected in their eyes is the
desire for something. They could move toward
each other. Their arms curling into each other.
They are filling their mouths with each other
and falling to the ground. They are rolling
over the warm ground making love…

—My little girl is at school.

—Where is her father? he asks.

Mickey brings them a stick.

-He died.

She did not want to say that. The dog drops a
stick at her feet and she picks it up again and
flings it high into the air. She follows it with
her eyes for a moment before bringing them back
to the young rider in her lawn.

She is very strong, he thinks to himself.

-So let's see this old bike, he says and
walks close to her, ready to follow.

-OK, she says after a heartbeat's pause. It's
in the garage.

She leads him across the gravel drive, away
from the house. He scans across the yard as
they walk. It is well kept. Already the lawn
has been trimmed close and cleaned of last
fall's leaves.

She bends down and lifts the aluminum door
easily to reveal a clutter of boxes, all marked
CLOSED. The boxes are in stacks, filling the
whole shed except for a space in the middle,
which has been kept open to make room for an
old vintage motorcycle. It is a Honda 350
with top pipes for on- and off-road driving. A
Scrambler.

The Honda is sleeping quietly, waiting to be
rediscovered, to be loved and taken care of.
The young rider smiles in spite of himself. He
crouches next to the old machine and the dog
immediately settles down next to him. He runs a
finger across the tank, through a layer of dust
revealing glittering gold paint.

-He took very good care of this, the rider
says, not taking his eyes off the metal curves
and angles. The engine case is clean, the chain
greased and the tires are new enough to be free
of any cracks or dry rot.

-You could probably get a little money for

it.

She doesn't respond. Only stands away, outside of the garage. His hand unconsciously opens above the head of the dog lying at his feet.

The rider pushes his hands against his knees and raises himself back to standing. He turns around to see clouds forming again over her shoulders. The house behind her is crowned in fast-moving nimbus clouds. He observes that these spring rains seem to be following him. He has no desire to spend the rest of the evening drenched atop a wobbling little bike.

-It's going to rain, he says, I have to get my bike and head out.

-You're going to ride in that? Her voice raises, alarmed.

He looks at her without asking for anything. Her face is full of welcome and hope. He wonders if she can read the fear in his eyes. It is not fear of the storm. It is fear of her. Fear of what she wordlessly offers him, under the now blustery canopy of newborn leaves in her front yard.

Sanctuary. Sanctuary from the storm, the road, the past, maybe even the future.

-Stay, she says. Go get your bike and stay. I'll make more room in here.

She pushes him aside and begins to move stacks of boxes closer together, toward the walls. He is about to speak, but he is interrupted by a heavy raindrop that hits him on the cheek just below his eye. The icy spark runs down his face and ends on his stubbled chin before he wipes it away with the back of his hand.

He doesn't think or speak. He looks up at the gathering clouds and begins to jog back down

the road toward his little green motorcycle.
Mickey is excited by this sudden movement and
the coming rain and begins to runs alongside of
him. The bouncing dog looks up and smiles at
this new man as if he was an old friend just
come home after a long journey.

Warmth rises from the earth. Body tucked in the cradle of a furrow between rows of tall corn. Through a thick canopy of sharp leaves and sticky tassels, white light cuts its way through every break in green. Impossible red-hot lances, crisscrossed and deadly, seek out purchase of flesh.

Contact is made: lightly scarred knee, the lower left ribs, newly swelling left breast, crown of the head, hair matted with dust and sweat.

Half a dozen or more. Each white tip penetrating through cloth or skin, through blood and bone, to pass through the body and pierce the soil underneath.

Laying, pinioned by light, unable to move. The traffic of insects below the canopy keeps to the cool channels of shadow. Wind wicks over the tops of the corn rows, unable to break into the density. The field only sways its vast body against the unyielding grip of roots to earth.

Drowning in the waves. Gasping for air. Suddenly standing, sending shards of broken light flying every which way. Pacing through shoulder length corn. North. South. East. West. Endless trembling rows.

Panic. Thirst. Vertigo. Gawky legs begin to run down long colonnades of supple stalks. White light shatters in hot bursts. Clods of clay-rich soil dryly explode underfoot. Heart race. The broad leaves reach down, giving paper-thin cuts in shoulder, shin, and cheek.

No end. Endless sentinel rows and an army of white lances in every direction. Each point is poised and every hot tip ready to impale.

Stop. Run. Gasping breath. Running again. Paper-thin cut. Stop. Scream. Unheard. Highway noise or wind. Run. Running. Tumbling over a furrow, crushing into towering stalks. Hot sky *bottlenecks at the hole. Threatens. Consumes. Gives life. Submit. Tears fall. Alone. Lost. Alone. Lost.*

Lost.

Lying down again. Crying breaths subside. The rows of corn shudder. Insects twitter. Hungry white light soothes and settles. Breathing easy. Euphoric. Seduced by helplessness. Green waves crash over a trembling child lying prone and open on a bed of fertile soil.

YOU LOST... ME

Dreams of a strange child possessed of powerful magics linger on the footsteps of waking. The images are still vivid, and when my eyes open I can see the small wicked girl levitating in front of a mirror more as memory than dream. She was a dangerous child, intoxicated by a power she did not understand. The child of my lover whose face I can't remember.

The light again carves a rough highway across my plastic woven carpet. I look at my bed. It is made and clean. The pillows are undisturbed at the head and the comforter is folded over at the corners. My grandmother would be proud.

"Emile." Her name floats in my head. I jump up to scan the room. There are teacups and empty bowls, sticky spoons and cigarette butts. Evidence. That was no dream.

Where is she? What is her phone number? I piece together our bizarre conversation, the tiny details of her departure, and there is nothing. She left behind no clue of where she lived, no scrap of information.

Presumably she lives in New York. But what if she's leaving? What if she is moving, or going home to her parents? I think she is a Brooklyn transplant, like me, but I don't know where she is from. Maybe she is going to fling herself off some bridge. Jesus.

I have to find her.

I slip on my shoes and my yellow knit stocking cap. I open the door to be buffeted by a huge blast of cold air. Halted by the wind, I listen for once to what is right in front of my face and I close the door.

My heart is pounding. Marching back into my room I kneel at the foot of my bed and slide out my full-length mirror. Leaving it on the floor, I stand above it and look at myself. I see a towering, unshaven, coatless man with wild eyes, wearing a T-shirt.

I realize I have to be at work again tonight. I look at the clock. It is 2:00 p.m. I have slept through most of the afternoon. My desk is cluttered with unopened mail and there is a gaping hole in the drywall below it where the power outlet from my computer has been torn half out of the wall.

-OK. OK. OK. She knows where I live. She will come back.

The man in the mirror is talking up at me, talking me down.

-Shower, make coffee, get it together and go to work.

This almost makes sense but there is an empty feeling in my stomach and an aching in my chest. I think I can save that woman. I think she can save me.

I have to find her.

Exhale.

I pick up the bowls and teacups, fill them with water and leave them in the sink. It is the day after Christmas. I look again at my room and my life. I don't like what I see here but there is a glimmer of possibility. She said she thought she was a ghost but I know she was real. There is a chance. There is hope.

The rough storm is causing the trees outside the little house to sway in unison, as if in the act of some dark evocation. The noise and the lightning is no longer disturbing the young man, nor the mother and child. They sit comfortably on the couch as the storm moves quickly above them. A five-year-old girl leans sleepily against him. The curls of her auburn hair tickle the skin of his arm. Her little stomach moves in and out with the breath of half sleep.

The hours had passed easily with a warm meal followed by a game of Yahtzee. The young girl had warmed quickly to the man and they found themselves laughing together as the storm chanted and guffawed outside. The woman and her daughter shared an infectious belly laugh, which the young man gratefully found disarming.

The woman sits on an overstuffed recliner, her legs wrapped underneath her, with Mickey curled on the ground below her. The little girl is curling deeper and deeper into his lap as she falls asleep.

-I think she might be ready for bed, the young man whispers.

He had talked and laughed so much this evening that his throat is sore and his voice comes out gravely. Titan had done most of the talking the night before and the young man had not found much other cause for talking since he had been on the road. This evening had felt good. Elise was an eager listener.

The woman starts to reach for the girl, to shake her awake, but the man waves her off, and lifts the little girl into his arms, and stands waiting for direction. Elise smiles as the little girl burrows herself into his arms.

-You should stick around, Tom. I think she likes you.

Something flashes in his eyes and she quickly turns to lead him to the child's room. She opens the door and pulls back bed sheets depicting a horse ranch. Cowboys with lassos are leaning gingerly on fence posts with sticks of hay in their mouths. He lays her down gently to find her hand gently clutching his shirtsleeve. He has to pull her fingers away to free himself before he steps away from the bed. Through the window above her bed he can see the storm has moved past them and is flashing in the distance.

-She is beautiful, he says, and quickly turns back into hall.

It is a moment before the woman joins him back in the living room. This time she sits next to him on the couch. There is space between them, but the weight of their bodies on the old cushions pulls them into the center of the couch. Two big invisible hands float in the room, squeezing them slowly together.

There is a new silence in the room, with the storm passed.

-Where are you going, Tom?

He thinks for a moment. He has only a tent, tied to his motorcycle. He is desperately broke. There is not even enough money in his wallet to get himself back home. He realizes in that moment that he has already passed the point of no return. Perhaps the steel bridge was the moment, the mile marker where he could have turned around with just enough gas to pull safely back into the drive of his mother's house. This trip would just have been an easy ride. The first ride of the season, to still his mind and ease his worries. He could have just gone home and salvaged something.

-I don't know, Elise. I think I will know when I find it.

She is looking deep into him. She is searching. She is openly hoping. The space between them shrinks to inches. His eyes clip across the room over the plants and the crayons. There is a bookshelf with books and a well-used wooden coffee table.

Quietly Elise says,

−Maybe you've found it.

He takes three short breaths, then speaks.

−I have a daughter as well, Elise. She is with my mother. Her name is Hollie. I have a son too... Tommy. I lost my, ah... There was a tent in our back yard. She... My... I watched the snow falling and... the tent turned into an igloo. It's just. I just. I can't...love again. I'm sorry.

He stands up. He touches her shoulder and gives her a soft squeeze. She opens her mouth to speak and nothing comes. Her hand is held gently over her chest as if carrying a small bird.

With his jacket and his boots on he steps outside into the night air. It is thick with moisture and very cool. He lets the air fill his lungs for a moment before walking across the drive to the garage. He quickly pulls open the garage door and rolls his motorcycle out onto the driveway. He scans the dark garage: piles of boxes marked CLOSED and a golden Honda that has been very well cared for. He looks up to the house to see curls of red hair silhouetted by the light of an interior hallway. He closes the garage gently and pushes his bike onto the road. He walks for a while with the bike, away from the house, before striking the engine and pulling off down the dark country road.

On the floor, lying on my stomach, the spit drying on my hand begins to chafe my dick. Emile.

   -*Unghh* is my frustrated grunt. I am humping my hand roughly on the hard floor and just giving myself blue balls. I can't do it. I feel guilty. My imagination has no business pouring over her body. I have been at this for an hour, a frustrating wrestling match with my own disfigured libido and a blurred sense of hope.

   I can see her in my mind and I have grown lustful and insane. I can see the two of us clawing into each other. I submit to her as she presses her whole weight into my chest. I can not. Cannot. Cum.

   I am a monster.

   Where is she? It has been almost a week since our evening together. I roll over onto my back and look at the imperfections of my ceiling. It is not spackled or textured in any way so the waves and cracks seem to press toward me when my landlord walks above me.

   The darkness outside is taunting me and I want to walk back to the Pulaski Bridge. Maybe she is there looking for me. I have been there four times already. On the subway I thought I saw her in a car ahead of me. I pushed through the crowd toward the door to pass between the cars. Just before I reached the door a group of slouching teenagers pushed through the doors from the adjacent car. They lumbered toward me, an unsatisfied, volatile wall. They each glared at me as I tried to crawl past them. As the train pulled into the Third Avenue station, the side doors opened just as I finally pushed into the next train car. She was not there, leaning with her face against the stainless steel pole as I thought I'd seen her. Seven or eight groping hands had replaced the dark bangs hanging over thick eyebrows. I was possessed with the impulse to escape the train immediately and I lunged out of the train toward the platform. The doors started to slam shut and I threw myself between them. They closed down on my chest and I was held there trapped until they snapped open and closed again, giving me time to fall out onto the platform. When I stood up and feverishly searched the platform, it was all but empty. She was nowhere to be seen.

I look down at my limp penis. Why is it a penis when it is flaccid and a cock when it is tumescent?

Shaking my head, I zip it back into my pants. I have a pillow on the floor and my reading lamp. There is a pile of paper and stubs of pencil. I have tried unsuccessfully to draw her face, again and again. It is always lopsided and I cannot draw hair. I have one drawing of an eye that I think is hers. She is slipping away.

Fuck.

A lamp over a garage door has attracted swarms of June bugs and mosquitoes. The lamp passes by him, leaving a momentary tail. A bullet tracer of memory-light. Suddenly he was a boy running through the sticky neighborhood of his grandmother, playing Ghosts and Goblins. He couldn't remember how the game worked, exactly, but there was singing in a circle. He remembered crouching behind a thick bush to hide. He had been a small boy and could fit himself into unreachable little spots in the yard. Being small made him good at the hide-and-seek games they played from dusk till full night. The children of the neighborhood played until the voices of their elders called, beckoning them home for sleep and adventurous dreams.

It seems that children play alone less these days. In his mother's neighborhood there is some new worry in the hearts of parents that keeps their children from running wild under the streetlights and shadows. "Not without supervision," his sister had said of her two small boys, who had now grown to the age where their urge for exploration was developing. This hadn't made sense because in his most cherished memories of her, she was a rowdy tomboy running free through fields and wild forests. Every day they would be shooed out of the house to find themselves on a grand adventure. His sister loved monarchs. She would catch them by the hundreds and hold them captive, as they epileptically fluttered inside a dark moist cardboard box. He would watch in awe as she would drag the box into an open meadow and let them free en masse. He could picture her alone on the fringes of a cornfield, spinning with her arms outstretched amid a kaleidoscope of silky butterfly wings.

His attention snaps back to the highway. Riding this late at night, his mind keeps drifting away from the road. The lights of his dials pulse green, making him think of driving cross-country with his father through long overnighters in the old Buick Skylark. Occasional streetlights remind him of crawling out of his mother's tiny basement window and prowling around the neighborhood. The moon is poised in the sky above him. Driving under the moon causes him to recollect the first time he had driven in a car without an adult. A friend of his, whose name he had forgotten, had just gotten a used yellow Chevette, which he called The Duck. He had snuck out of the house and climbed in the car at 4:00 a.m. He and his nameless friend drove all the way to Norfolk, looking for a meteor shower.

He needs to stay focused. He needs to look for pairs of glowing eyes. Signs for Deer Crossing appear every ten miles or so. But the signs only bring him back to a late-night drive home with his sister when they were teenagers. She was a few years younger than he and it was her job to stay awake and watch for deer. He had kept her attention by telling her of a girl lost in a wilderness of magic and darkness. Though he can remember nothing else of the story he knows he had held her captivated.

He doesn't think of the little girl and her red-haired mother cuddled in a bed. They are already a hundred miles behind him. He doesn't think that he could also be enveloped in the warmth of their arms. Thoughts of his own daughter strike him like a hammer in the chest. He doesn't think of his wife incoherently babbling in a hospital bed. He avoids all those thoughts. It is too painful and he has spent the last two years in the grips of that pain.

He journeys back through the joy of his life. The mile markers slip by numberlessly and he lets his mind wander from the road upon which he is currently throttling. Instead he travels down the roads of his childhood. His memories all seem to have a vibrating glow around them, a kind of mind aura. As if his memories are protected or sacred and safe from any tarnish.

He sinks into the saddle of his motorcycle. His body is too numb to be bothered by the brisk air. He feels his mind settle deep in the comfort of those thoughts. He feels surrounded by this strange hushed sphere. He feels protected. There is no struggle as his eyes grow heavy and he slumps farther into the seat of the bike. It is almost natural. He and the bike are one and guide each other. The hum of the engine is muted and syncopates with the shuddering air around him. There is no struggle. Only safe sleep...as the bike continues its straight path down the country road.

Water from the ice bucket hoisted over my head drips onto my face as I huff up the stairs again. I have lost count of the trips back and forth from the bar upstairs. The place has been filled for hours with partiers pushing themselves into oblivion. There is something desperate and innocent in their effort to cauterize the last year of their lives, to nip last year's disappointment in the bud. It is an ugly and necessary ritual.

I push through bodies, the ice bucket held above their heads, balancing on my extended arms. Every inch is a push. The whole crowd is an orifice. People are overheating and layers of clothing are coming off and being thrown to the floor. Outside, the city is covered in black ice. Inside the people have vanished and there is only thigh and belt and nipple and hair and knuckles and hips.

Push through. I look up to see Mr. Bigshot, the owner, standing on the corner of the bar, conducting the zombie orchestra with his glass of vodka like Steamboat Mickey.

They love him. They are whipped into a frenzy as he climbs up onto a chair. I push through and make it behind the bar. J.B. is there grinning with creepy disdain. He is past cynical. His eyes focus on me hungrily through his cocaine haze and he hands me another shot of booze. One shot for each grueling sprint up the stairs.

-It's bad enough the fucking ice maker is in the basement, but there isn't much left. We are fucked! I am all but screaming over the music and the howling crowd.

We take the shot and spin back to work. I am his bar-back. I clean glasses and replace empty bottles of booze. I hold his head over the toilet when he's puking in the bathroom and I get him back behind the bar to serve drinks as dazzlingly and magically as always.

I love J.B., in spite of his attempts to get in my pants. I know he means well and he never lets this frustration get in the way of having a good time at work. I don't know if he hates women or queens more, but his loathing for both is palpable and he never hesitates to display it. I have seen him light a girl's hair on fire without her noticing, then jump to her rescue, dumping a pitcher of beer over her head. He is gay, but he says he is attracted to men, not fags. We have a certain amount of self-loathing in common and that's why we get along so well.

A hand slides under my ass, all the way to my balls, then gives me a little push. Without looking, I sidestep clear out of the way. This is Kylie's charming way of getting me to move out of her way. She's an older Australian woman, who spent most of her life touring the world as a model. She was on the cover of *Paris Vogue*. Now she is here with a push-up bra and sneakers, serving drinks to drooling young businessmen with cocaine hard-ons and glassy eyes.

Besides Frank, this is my closest New York family. I have been working here for two years. I bought my shoes with money I made from hauling ice for these drinks. I love the work, though. I've always felt work is easier to swallow than the rest of my life. Hard work is purifying.

Looking up over the crowd in their bloodlust, I am amazed that just a handful of us are able to control this mob. I see them rending each other's flesh in a bacchanalian orgy. They're close to going mad and devouring each other; I love it.

I put my head down and return to my mechanical dance. *Happy New Year, Thom!* My mind is half melted by booze. Only the repetition

107

of my movements keeps me standing. I am a machine. I try to focus on something. I don't know what it is. Something I want, something I am missing in all of this. Nothing forms. The desire remains shapeless and gives the easy conclusion: I don't want anything.

A sleek black ant makes an ascent along the hairline of his sticky forehead. The sun is cresting the horizon and warmth is quickly spreading over the rolling countryside. The modest range of the northern Appalachians hug the ground like a line of migrating gray buffalo.

Beads of sweat begin to form on his face. A few of the drops cascade down onto the ant, making the climb even more precarious. Something rich lies at the top of this man mountain. A ripe smell wafts from above and pulls the ant instinctively forward.

With an unconscious wipe and a jerk the rider sits half up. An immediate sense of danger is quickly dispelled by the warmth of the soft soil beneath him. A quick check of his body reveals he is all put together, save for a small scrape on the center of his forehead. A bit of dried blood and nothing more. His helmet is somehow cradled between his ankles.

Stiffly, he gets to his feet to see his motorcycle a few yards ahead of him. It is startling to see the bike lying on its side. It looks heavy and inert. The handlebars are twisted rudely to one side giving the impression of a broken neck. He lifts the bike up and pulls it back onto the center stand. The ground is relatively smooth here. They must've slipped off the road, rolled through the shallow ditch and just coasted into this old barren cornfield.

He shakes his head.

-Stupid.

He tries to remember the drive last night, his wavering headlight, the cool night air. No moment or thing sticks out in his mind. He thinks he drove through most of the night. There is still a bit of gas in the tank, which is lucky. He isn't stranded, not yet.

He leaves the bike for a moment to hike back up to the road. There are no cars, and the morning sun catches the asphalt in its glow and stretches back the way he came like a golden serpent. Across the road there is another embankment. This ditch is much deeper and a small post fence runs along its rocky bottom. He would be dead if he had gone off of that side. The countryside is turning into foothills and the road is becoming slightly more perilous here. Occasional switchbacks and rolling hills carve through a rocky landscape with only patches of farmlands or fields. He has left the Great Plains behind.

Turning around, he looks back down the easy slope to his bike and scattered belongings. Everything is accounted for and looks to be in pretty good shape. With a shrug he dismisses the insanity of passing out on the bike, rolling comfortably into an empty field and sleeping through the night without so much as a headache to pay.

He dusts himself off, straightens his crooked rearview mirrors, reties his bag to the bike, and straps his helmet tightly around his chin. He pushes the bike off its stand and gently turns the engine over with the kick-start. The battery was left on through the night so he is afraid he'll have to push it up the hill to the road in order to push-start the bike.

To his surprise, after a chug and a hiccup, the bike comes awake after the first kick. He pats the dusty green tank with affection and rides the bike gently up the hill and back onto the twisting road. He has been heading east for a few days now. Although he's been in no hurry and the country highways make for a leisurely pace, he has come quite a distance.

A few miles down the road he comes to a crossroads town with a gas station. He fills up the bike and grabs a plastic-wrapped coffee cake from the counter. It is well before noon and there is a nice cool breeze in the air. He looks down the road to the rising foothills growing into mountains looming in the distance.

Northward the road stretches as far as the eye can see into a broad valley land. With nowhere for him to be and just a pocket full of dollar bills, the less dramatic roads seem more appealing. Usually the mountains would draw him eagerly with the promise of hairpin turns and breathtaking vistas. Today, the rider turns north. Not sure what he is looking for, he is doing the best he can to calm the chatter of his worried mind. He heads down the road, away from the beautiful mountains. This is, after all, no joy ride.

A crooked arm lies across my chest. Our bodies are uncovered and I follow the slopes and shallows of her back with my eyes. Her skin has dried somewhat in the morning air. My back is warm and moist on the bedside. I am growing uncomfortable, but I don't want to move. Her ass is exposed and her long legs stretch easily to the end of the bed.

Kylie is a tall woman, easily taller than me. She seems to like me. I don't think she actually cares. Not that we aren't friends, I just think she loves sex and is lonely. I am occasionally convenient because I am an easy indiscretion.

As to why I am having sex with her, I don't know. Where is Emile? I haven't stopped searching for her. I haven't stopped thinking about her. Sex with Kylie doesn't mean anything; it's just an empty encounter. It doesn't feel like an act of aggression. Sex is just satisfying a necessity.

The clarity with which I am gazing around the room is incredible considering how much alcohol I consumed last night. I don't usually get that drunk at work, but evidently I sweated out the worst of it.

I try to move and she digs her nails into my chest.

-Don't even think about it, Thommy Boy.

-I have to go, I snort back.

-That is bullshit, Kylie snarls back, we have the night off.

-I know. I know. I'm catching my words because Kylie has never been precious or cared about me hanging around. This is a surprise. She wants me to stay, snuggle, for us to spend the day together. She wants something. I don't have a response.

-We could give it another go at least? she says softly.

Rather than respond, I just pull my body roughly from underneath her and slide off the bed. I pull my pants on and look at her again. She is gorgeous, easily one of the most attractive women I've ever been with. She is probably ten years older than me, but that doesn't matter. She is in better shape than me. Her limbs are long and athletic. She has lines in her eyes, but it gives the impression of having traveled across the world rather than getting older. She is sexy.

Kylie doesn't move or say anything else. I am surprised. I think I've hurt her feelings. Quickly finishing getting dressed, I almost lean back over and kiss her, but I hesitate, then don't. It would just be condescending.

-Have a good day, Kylie, is all I say.

She doesn't answer. Her eyes are closed. I turn to go and I can feel them on my back. I am out the door, down the stairs, and on Prince Street in SoHo surrounded by hundreds of pedestrians: shopping, gawking, or just being seen. There are models everywhere. In this part of the city they tower over the tourists strutting down the concrete runway. They are gods in this neighborhood and stumble around on their platform shoes like a Greek chorus, eager for laudations.

I walk quickly and invisibly through the churning crowd. I skip down the subway stairs to a crowded platform. The white tiled walls are decorated with little mosaic people carrying umbrellas and bowling balls. The little people are all connected by a rough black line of stone or something, a dark river flowing through them.

A train barrels into the station and people crowd toward it as it screeches to a halt.

113

I squeeze in as the door closes us all in together. So many people are out today. New Year's Day. My head has finally started to ache a bit, but not too badly.

Hundreds of people enter and leave the train at each station as I follow its course to Brooklyn. The landscape of faces constantly shifting. I keep an eye out for Emile in the tide. Looking for a ghost is vaguely unsettling, but I think it imbues the train car with a kind of social memory. The train travels along on its rails with humans coursing in and out of it like blood being distributed to the extremities of the larger body of the city. The train knows where she is. The train can feel me pensively watching.

My head shakes vaguely against the glass of the door. I am not sad, I decide. I realize I should not have slept with Kylie. It felt OK at the time, but it is not what I want. It isn't real. An empty feeling sits in my chest. A deep longing. If I could just find Emile, we could leave this city together and have a real life. That is what I am feeling. Hope smashing up against delusion.

The train stops at my station and I briskly push out the turnstiles and jog up the stairs. The street is much more sparse here in Brooklyn. A few hipsters and blue-collar Latinos. Teenagers roam around aimlessly in packs.

I shove my hands in my pockets and feel for the money I made last night. Several hundred bucks, easily. Good timing for the rent. I turn the corner to my building and all but run over Gina. She has her blue coat on.

-Hey watch it! Oh. She recognizes me and smiles.

I half expect her to make an overture, but she just ambles over to the deli. She looks

114

rested and showered. She obviously is not working today. She isn't even bothering to collect aluminum cans.

As I turn back around I notice a handful of dead reeds with fragile florets jutting out of the cracks at the base of a street pole. I crouch down and run my fingers across their empty seedpods. The winter somehow did not tear these dead stalks from their roots and I have not noticed them before. Without knowing why, I pull them gently out of the ground and go inside my apartment. It is a relief to be home. I don't feel anxious about my lack of plans this evening. Not content, not anxious. I place the handful of dead stalks on my coffee table and sit quietly on the floor next to them.

Peanut butter crackers and a half tank of gas.

Outside there's no wind and the sun is gently draped by wisps of cirrus clouds. He is leaning against the bike looking northward up the winding road ahead. There is a furrow in his brow. An onlooker might think he was lost deep in thought. Not true though. His body is slightly taut and as he chews the crackers a muscle emerges rhythmically from his jaw.

Like the mare's-tail clouds cruising across the sky, his mind is flying above the road. The sky took a laughing course northward over the path still untraveled, a lovely place for the old motorcycle to end its journey. It found an ornery trucker to get the rider farther down the road. It watched each footstep on the black asphalt. A sunrise and a sunset in a single day, a solitary young man, running away to deliver salvation.

The rider shakes his head and all the tension leaves his body. He comes back into himself and out of his daze. His mind had blankly wandered.

-I must be dehydrated, he says to himself. He steps back into the gas station to ask if there is a water fountain. The clerk shakes his head and points to a grimy toilet in the back of the store.

The fluorescent lights delay for a moment after he flips the switch before they crackle on, revealing a greasy sink and a toilet that has not been flushed. The rider lifts his boot and kicks the lid of the seat up. A novelty machine is hung on the wall above the toilet. As he stands to pee, at eye level he sees a busty woman on a motorcycle advertising a ROUGH RIDE. The condom machine is asking for a dollar for a condom and possibly some lube. In spite of its absurdity, he finds himself staring at the little cartoon woman.

His crotch has been aching from the constant

buzz of the saddle and suddenly the breasts of the busty cartoon woman begin to rise and fall, as if she is gently breathing. He feels himself getting unexpectedly erect. Embarrassed and frustrated, he starts massaging his dick quickly while leaning over the fetid toilet. He can see himself in the mirror, but he tries not to look there. His eyes have sunk back into his head a little and his skin is stretched tight over his cheeks.

He is getting close and begins to breath heavily when there is a loud knock on the door.

-You gonna be all day? an impatient voice barks.

Shocked and ashamed, the rider doesn't respond. He quickly zips up his jeans, turns the water on, and takes a quick drink from the faucet. With his head down he pushes through the door of the station and goes directly to his bike. He hears the gruff voice call from inside the store,

-Can't ya flush, ya *asshole*?

The rider says nothing in response. He uncomfortably sits on his bike, puts the key in the ignition, fires it up, and takes off down the road.

Growing piles of scrawl begin to clutter my apartment. Sketches on loose-leaf paper spill off my table and onto my floor. My vacant bed has become a mosaic of eyes and ears. Weeks have passed and I cannot shake Emile from my consciousness. Nor can I seem to put back together her unusual features with paper and pencil. Day after day the memory of her becomes more and more piecemeal. The details of her face dissolve into gray shapes, sharp lines, only to deteriorate into ideas: sorrow, hunger, annihilation, lust. Then her face becomes simply moonlight, water, cool breeze, a dark pool.

My room smells musty and slightly fecund. I have begun a collection. Dried stalks of weeds, harvested off the city's skin. I am not looking for them, but I've begun to notice them everywhere: under the subway pylons, or at the base of the Brooklyn Bridge. These are the last remnants of last year's urban wild growth.

They are long dead and dried and the collection is vaguely macabre. My room is filled with dead flowers, like a forgotten mortuary or the bedroom of teenager fallen prey to unrequited love. The weather is already changing, and sprouts of new things are pushing once again through the thawed concrete. My collection of dried urban foliage satisfies exactly what I am missing here. It is evidence of life, tiny sentinels of the struggle of nature against the tide of cement and hedge funds. Each day I find another dried stalk and draw it. Drawing has become my way to bear witness to Emile.

Sharpening what is left of my pencil, I gather up my studies. The drawing of mouth and eyelid intermingle with pistil and stem. I feel a new rhythm in my chest. The result of my ongoing hermitage is a meditative heart-thrum so loud it breaks the quiet of my room and syncopates with the distant subway.

I sit frozen over a blank piece of paper. I stare at a bundle of dried foliage plucked from sacred rings hidden in unnoticed corners of the vast city. I look backward into the days when these plants were sticky and green, trembling in the wind alongside rushing vehicles and numberless indifferent footfalls.

My pencil hits the paper with a scrape. My hands are clenched tightly and move quickly across the page. There is something there, something I see now, that I have been struggling for. I draw for an hour or more and stop abruptly. Nothing is finished. None of my drawings are, but this drawing has suddenly frustrated me. I can render an object with some skill, but have never been able to draw from memory. I cannot seem to hold on to an image or a memory for very long. My mind has never been still enough.

I look out my window, and the tiniest leaves are showing their first buds. Green.

I need paint. I don't usually paint, so I don't have any. Evening is approaching and the streets will start to fill up again soon. The last place on earth I want to be is on Bedford Avenue among the affected and afflicted hipsters, sucking off Brooklyn's tit.

I am no different, except perhaps I use my teeth.

-OK. I have to get paint.

I get off the floor. My body has grown accustomed to living on the rough carpet. It has toughened me up a little. My body isn't sore, or lethargic. It feels full of power.

When I open the door, however, my heart drops. The wind is brisk and there are children bicycling across the street, in and out of an empty warehouse. The children are laughing and screaming. I am afraid they will notice me. I imagine them circling me on their bicycles, jeering at me like I'm a hunchback.

My nerve endings feel bare and exposed. I hunch my shoulders and hurry past them. I see my reflection in a car window and I have to laugh. I am too boyish and pretty to be taken seriously by anyone. I just look hip.

The world is perfect. There is no wind. The sky is bright. Something like rebirth is in the air. Spring has finally fixed its grip on the land and promised forgiveness and redemption.

His gas runs out.

He knew it was coming. The motorcycle sings its chugging song, eager to continue moving forward but choking on sparkless oxygen, dies. It loses speed and he coasts for a hundred yards or so. As it slows to a halt, he pulls it gently to the side of the road and dismounts.

He stands there silently for a long time, during which no cars pass. There is only the faintest breeze, a distant highway hum, and the ticking and chirping of the cooling engine. Heat rises from the engine and oil still percolates through the bike's arteries. The bike is old and well loved. Its emerald green tank is faded and dented slightly but retains the simple dignity of a small engine, late seventies, Universal Japanese Motorcycle.

He begins to untie his bag and gear from the rear of the bike. It is not a heavy load, a weather-beaten red backpack, filled mostly with socks and a small tent from Walmart. He hangs his helmet on the handle bars and takes a step away from the bike.

He wants to hug it, or say something. He looks up at the sky, then to the distant tree line. Everything is perfect.

He reaches out until his fingers just touch the tank, then turns and starts walking down the road. He started this little journey riding with a bike as his only companion and it seems now he will have to finish the journey alone and on foot.

The boots he received from Titan and Old Lady are snug and comfortable enough. His body feels strange walking, however. It is still vibrating in unison with the machine. His blood is pumping like oil and thoughts ricochet like sparks across contact points. His hips roll like a camshaft, pushing his feet methodically forward.

He stops suddenly in the road and turns back to look at the bike. It is a few yards back, patiently waiting to be filled with gas and ridden again.

-This is stupid, he says loudly. What if someone comes along and has gas or a truck? What if some one picks us up?

He decides he can at least push the bike for a while. He had been thinking a long time about the inevitability of running out of money and therefore gas. He had planned on just walking from then on. But now, he was faced with the reality of just leaving the bike on the road and walking on, with nothing, toward nothing.

He did not know where he would be when it happened, only that it would, and here he is. And in this moment he realizes that this little motorcycle that he spent three weeks rebuilding under the watchful eyes of his elder machinist friend, Andreas, is the last thing he really possesses. If he decides to go without it, he will have walked away from everything. That realization suddenly fills him with an unexpected and overwhelming sadness. Words come out from the man,

-This is real. This is my life. This is me. This is my choice.

His voice does not crack or break. It is quiet and humble and firm.

He turns his back to the motorcycle and all the road behind him. He begins to walk down the highway, on a beautiful afternoon.

I am standing outside Dumont. The streetlights
are on already, although the sky is still light
blue. Through the window I see booths filled
with young people, looking beautiful and eating
truffled risotto and skate meunière. The sun is
beginning to come down over the Brooklyn-Queens
Expressway. It is warm enough for a T-shirt and
there are swaths of skin filling my eyes.

An intoxicating air wafts from the
restaurant. Again I see my reflection in the
glowing windows, smoking and bedraggled. This
is my first foray "out" in weeks. Frank is
either not here yet or he is already sitting in
the patio in back.

After another drag, I flick my cigarette
butt into the gutter and open the door. I
am met by a drunkenly animated and smiling
group of hipsters making their way out of the
restaurant, so I step to the side and wait. I
am nestled in the corner of the doorway, which
is half covered in a velvety curtain, and a
woman with her hair shaved tight makes eye
contact with me. Her eyes are watery and it
doesn't seem she's with the rest of the crowd.
I smile at her weakly and she just turns her
head to the sidewalk and is gone.

Inside, I can hear chic and mournful
DeVotchKa in the background singing, "and you
alllllllready know…how this willll end" and
I am suddenly glad I agreed to meet Frank. I
nod past the maitre d' and point with my index
finger toward the patio. I move through the room
quickly and with ease. I may have become a
recluse, but I can still navigate a scene.

Frank is at the bar in the back, already with
a drink. He is craning his neck back when I
walk in and immediately he is off his stool.

Frank is beaming, electrified by the crowd.
All the energy of New York City in the spring
is being channeled into Dumont and through

Frank. He is a creative monolith with boundless energy. He is my best friend.

I know I am at least one of his closet friends. He is friends with everyone though, the grocer, the tailor, the mayor. Frank is Brooklyn's ambassador to Texas and the rest of the free world. "Best friend" is obnoxious. To him, I am a half-brother and he has a lot of other brothers and sisters. He is my best friend because I am less socially agile. Less sure of myself.

-Thom! Where have you been?

He speaks over the crowd and beckons for me to sit. I join him at the bar and he orders me a beer, a Javier.

We sit in silence as the bartender swiftly pulls a glass off the shelf and fills it from the tap. The bartender has tattooed arms and wields them like loaded weapons, full of power and purpose. I look a few seats down the bar and see a girl staring at the bartender. Her index finger is resting on her lower lip, pulling it open slightly. She feels my gaze and catches me spying on her spying. It is embarrassing for us both, so I don't look at her again.

-Thom? Where have you been?

Frank has a lot he wants to say. He wants to catch up, get the ball rolling, get to work, spar, tango, fight, whatever, but he wants to talk.

I don't have an immediate answer so I just look at my beer. I am holding it, I realize. It's in my hand. I should drink it.

The beer is golden under the string of patio lights. It looks like a magical object.

-Thom, man, we have been missing you. There is so much going on, I mean J.H. and I are

really on to something and we are hoping to
have a reading soon. There is a part for you
man, a good one. The reading is only gonna
be for us, you know, we need more time, but
you should audition for it when we shoot. You
have to! And Kate is pissed you missed writing
group. You can't just not show up. I have to
like "report" on what happened now. I mean
fuck. You know, who cares, but you know what
happened? I just saw Ryan's new show, are you
going to see it? Thom. You have to. You have to
see it. From the opening moment, it just… Thom,
I have to seriously rethink what theater even
is to me now. *Mind-blowing!* We are definitely on
board with Ryan. See it. What are you reading?
Did you finish *The Brothers Karamazov* yet? Isn't
it the best? He just sits there across from
Christ and says "get lost," you know. It is so
perfect. I am reading DeLillo. He's got it man,
he is *the* American voice.

I take a drink of the beer. It is gold.
Magic, even. The beer hits my eyeteeth and
sends a shock to my temples. It is liquid shock
therapy. The lights on the patio pulse with the
music. The noise of the crowd ebbs and flows
like someone is fucking with the volume on the
god-mike.

-I think I have to go, Frank, I'm sorry.

-What? *Why?* Thom, we haven't even ordered, I
mean, are you OK?

If I had a shovel and enough time to dig a
little cave under this bar and talk to Frank
through a little pipe. I think that would be
OK.

-I am fine, Frank, I'm just tired.

-Well, wait Thom, wait. I mean, where have
you been? What's happening?

The noise of plates being slid across a
stainless steel counter top cuts through the

noise of the bar; I am lying on the tarmac at JFK, looking up at the stars, as a plane is coming in on top of me.

-I think I fell in love. I don't know. I just can't talk about it now. I am looking for her. It just feels right. Can we go?

Frank stares flatly at me. He starts to say something more, then just shakes his head. His head drops a little, as if resigned, than snaps up again.

-No, Thom. This is just not good enough.

His voice is level. He is calm and focused.

-Thom, this is very disrespectful. To all of us. We have invested so much in each other. To just push that away… I… I just can't believe it. You started the writing group. So much work has come of that. You're in love? Fine. Great, can't wait to meet her, but where are *you*? Where is Thom? You are scaring me. Just give me a rea—

My voice cuts into his with the gravity of a full sack of coins.

-No. I can't.

Something like time passes between us.

-OK, Thom. OK.

His voice is almost a whisper. He is truly hurt. There is something I want to say but can't because I don't know what it is because I haven't found it. Right now it doesn't matter. I have said what's important.

He gets up and leaves.

I sit there a moment. I am still holding the beer. It is warmer now. Moisture is forming in the creases of my hand. I raise the glass to my lips and take a long drink. It goes down bitter.

I feel eyes on me and glance back over my shoulder. The girl with eyes for the bartender now has eyes for me. I look back at my glass, now half empty.

OK.

I finish the beer and ask the bartender to put her drink on my tab and to close it up.

I spin on my stool her way.

-Wanna get out of here?

-Totally.

She grabs her purse and pulls down her short black spandex skirt as she slides off the barstool. We are pushing out the dining room and then I see Her. My drawings of nose, lip, collarbone, eye, all coming together at the same place at the same time right in front of me.

We are right on top of her table when I notice Emile. I also take in the sporty-looking man she's with and the wedding ring on her hand. I am not certain if I noticed that before. Is it new? Did I just not notice a huge wedding ring? Emile is sitting right here with this man who is wearing a simple golden band on his ring finger. Their hands are extended toward each other on the table but not touching.

She looks up at me and at first there is nothing, then a startled look, then sorrow, then a grimace, and then she turns her head away from me.

I am pushed outside by my intrepid new friend in the miniskirt. There is noise and silence. I light a cigarette and look off toward Frank's house. My new friend is shifting on her hips, waiting. I take a drag and say,

-You know when you get an arm cut off? You're supposed to still feel it, like a phantom limb or something? I think I am that. I mean, I have that. Emotionally.

   -Cool, She says.

   -Do you want to grab a drink?

He has not gone far. A mile. The first truck that passes slows. The sound of engine braking cracks into the air and the semi pulls off the road ahead of him. He did not have a thumb out. He was not waving or even looking for a ride.

And here is a ride, so he jogs up behind the big rig and pulls himself up into the cab.

-Hey there bud. Saw ya there, thought you may need a lift.

The driver is a big man with blondish hair and a wispy unkempt beard. On his right hand the faded scrawl of a ballpoint reads MOM'S BIRTHDAY.

-I'm Samuel.

-Well, thanks for the lift. My name is Tom.

-Where ya headed?

-Just headed, Samuel.

They shake hands and Samuel throws the rig back into gear. He pulls back onto the road raising a cloud of gravel and dust as he throttles the rig back up to speed.

-You got a long way yet. Not a whole heck of a lot going on in this neck of the woods. Just headed, huh? The old walkabout. Good time of year for that. Bit chilly at night yet, but the sun's starting to feel real good. I am doing the long haul: California to Maine, so you can come along as far as you please.

In the cabin of the truck, the air is thick with a rubbery smell. Layers of sweat on dried vinyl. The young hitchhiker does not respond. He only nods his head, thinking of Maine. Lobsters and deep forest. Maine would be a good place to start over.

The cab of the truck is high off the ground and the young man is a bit unsettled by the rhythmic bouncing motion. Walking was just

beginning to feel natural again. He could have
walked for a couple of days and covered ten
or twenty miles. It would be much easier to
lie back in this rolling pitch with the high
whine of gears. He can feel vibrating beneath
his boots. Two days of driving and he could
just step out of the truck and be in Maine.
Trees are starting to sparsely line the road
and hills are breaking up the horizon. The
hills are rolling into the distance, building
momentum to blow into foothills and bluffs and
finally buttes and mountains.

-Can you make any animal noises?

Samuel has an easy grin filled with straight,
bright teeth. He continues,

-I like to make a bit of a racket here in
this cab. Just to pass the time, you know? I'm
known for it. I can do a real good cat and bark
like a whole pack of pooches. I like little dog
noises better than big dog noises, you know?
Couldn't bring a big dog with me in the truck
really so I make them little dog noises. Rarf!

He yelps.

It sounds a good deal like a small dog
getting his tail stepped on. Samuel is pleased
with the sound and his head shakes rhythmically
side-to-side as if there is a happy song being
played in his mind.

-Pretty good, huh? Ha! I got that one down
good. I can do some tougher ones: Duck makes
some good sounds and piglets is fun and a
rabbit will scream like a banshee if it thinks
it's gonna get ate up. You ever heard that
noise?

The young man thinks he has. His childhood
cat, Tiger, had brought a live rabbit into
the house and he could remember the sound the
rabbit made just before Tiger finally ended its
life under the stairs. It filled the house. It

130

overwhelmed the TV upstairs and the washing machine next to his room in the basement. It kept him from sleep that night. It rang in his ears for hours. It was a cry of mortal fright. Panic. Anguish.

-I ain't got that rabbit one down, though. I tried it in a diner in Silver Creek and the waitress next to me almost spilled a pot of coffee on this old bird. Noise wasn't right, though, and she got real mad. Said I had the Tourette's and had to shut it or leave. I'll get it down though. Love them sounds. Animal sounds. Not birds so much. A horse makes some good noises. And little noises, like a mouse noise.

Thus the now-hitchhiking young man is serenaded as he rumbles north toward Great Lakes, Appalachians, deep American forest, and lobsters.

The walls of her apartment are exposed brick. There is only one small room with a kitchen and an adjacent bathroom. I'm sitting on the bed watching her sway against the wall. I am drunk and my eyes want to close.

I stand up and face her. She has nothing to say. Her fingers are pressed into the wall behind her and her head is rolling back against the wall.

A TV noise filters through the bricks. It could be a game show or a shopping channel. The window is cracked, letting the street air into the room. I reach my hand up and trace the goose flesh on the inside of her arm.

I move in to kiss her neck and she pulls back. Her arm snaps up to my chest and pushes me away. We are close enough to smell the whiskey on each other's breaths. She does not look at me. Her face is turned into the wall. She pushes against me with her arm and digs herself into the bricks.

I take half a step backward and her pushing hand suddenly grabs up my shirt in a balled fist and roughly pulls me into her. I step toward her and she immediately begins to push against me again.

Slowly I take her arm by the wrist and pull her hand away from my chest and pin it to the wall above her head. I bite into her neck and she lets out an angry moan.

In a quick movement she pushes past me, toward the door, as if to escape. I grab her neck from behind with one hand and she stops. The tension melts out of her body and she presses herself into me. She slides herself down my chest and thighs.

Then she bolts again. But I have her. She struggles against my grip noiselessly. I have to control her arms with my hands because she is beginning to scratch me.

I am already breathing hard with the struggle. With a grunt I lift her into the air and lay her face down into the bed. I have her arms pinned with one hand and I use the other to pull her skirt up to her waist. She has nice lacy underwear on. Rather than tear it off I pull it down her otherwise bare legs.

She stops struggling for a moment and instead of kicking me in the face she steps gingerly out of her panties and flicks them into the corner with her high-heeled foot.

Then she fights me again. She shakes violently against my grip and gets one of her arms free. She reaches back and gives me a nasty rake across my bare neck. I let her go at me, tearing up skin and punching while I slip the belt off my pants.

Once I have the belt off I grab her by the waist, lift her off the bed and throw her back down onto her stomach. With one hand pushing down on her back, I lift my belt over my head and bring it down hard on her bare ass. She muffles a cry into her bed and her body stiffens beneath me.

Her struggling stops. Her legs inch subtly apart. I bring the belt down on her again. And again. With each strike her body softens more and she muffles a cry into her blankets. Two more hits and she lets out a loud cry. Her legs buckle, she is hanging limply off the side of the bed.

I move her hand from her back and drop the belt to the floor. I take my dick out and lift her by the hips roughly onto the bed. I push into her in one movement and her body coils in response. Coils to strike. With each stroke she claws, crawls, bites, strikes me.

I am too angry and too drunk to cum so I just keep fighting and fucking her. I think, this isn't going to stop.

And of course it stops. Her hands turn soft and my body hears this touch and we both become perfectly still. She slides away from me and curls herself up in a ball on her bed.

-Thank you, she says. You can go.

Black pits carved into sweaty white dice. Two pitch eyesockets staring into a cluttered room. Boxes. Fists of small cash. Knuckled cigarette butts.

Snake eyes.

Small fingers clutching trousers. Taut leg trembles beneath the pants. Nothing but stretched flesh to hold onto. Clutch the trousers.

Dense smoke clouds hang in a circle over popcorn dice. Stocky men steal pinches through a pretty red dress covered in bright yellow daisies. Beneath the pants the leg tightens further, jeered. Baited.

Dollar bills snatched away. Long stealing fingers find fresh leg-skin underneath yellow daises. Clutch the trousers. Elusive smoke pulled to and fro in the wake of angrily swinging arms.

The dice roll. Bullets up again. Snake eyes. There is laughter first. Then a deep shaking voice erupts.

Violence. Knives drawn to cut through indifferent smoke. From the trousers waves a shooting iron. Impenetrable. Focused. Tight legs tremble for a moment then become taut again.

The cigarette smoke is drawn to the gun and licks the lips of the barrel.

Cash falls in a pile, covering the lidless eyes of the dice.

Clutching still to the inside of trouser legs but gathering courage. Shoot. Shoot. Shoot. The room empties and becomes silent aside from hoarse breath from above.

The gun disappears again into the belt of the trousers and little hands collect greasy ones and fives. Picking sickly green daisies, leaving two beady snake eyes staring up from the floor.

-Smoke this.

Shallow pulls from a cigarette. The white paper curls slowly back. A little chimney at its end.

-Drink this.

A capful of hot burn and the little fingers are now clutching the slender body of a cigarette.

Stooping to pick up the dice, they are hurtled with too much gusto and pop across the wooden floor beams. Two black eyes. Snake eyes staring out, taking in the whole room. Their empty glare has found a bright red dress with cheaply printed yellow daisies.

-You lost.

Pulled back to oily trousers, now in a pile around thin white ankles. Taut legs. The shooting iron held. The smoke is drawn to it and dances in the corner of tiny pouting lips.

BREAKING OF THE SHELL

The rig pulls into a large gravel lot where there are a few other semis parked side by side. There is another parking lot closer to the brightly lit bar, The Office, which is filled mostly with pickup trucks and rust buckets. The southern shore of Lake Erie is just over the crest of a hill and a few patches of Canadian land separate the lake from Huron and Superior. The young man had come a long way from home.

Samuel is bouncing anxiously in his seat. His belly is a small protrusion bumping into the bottom of the steering wheel. The Office has always been a favorite stop along this route.

-Don't tell me you can't go in! I got the drinks, brother. We've been in the barn for hours! Let me get you one. It's karaoke!

The young man's lips are tightly pursed. He doesn't move for a moment. He is a full suitcase left forgotten on a busy train platform.

-OK, he says, I would take you up on some

chicken fingers maybe.

-Woo-*hoo*! Samuel hoots.

Samuel throws wide the door of the cab and scampers down the side of the rig. He is almost skipping across the gravel toward the inviting noise of the bar.

The young man moves slower. He struggles against the weight of the door. There is a cool breeze that sneaks into every crease of his jacket. His knees half buckle when his feet hit the ground. Vertigo and a skunky smell picked up by the wind strike his temples. He gives his head a shake and wobbles across the lot toward the bar.

Samuel holds the door for the young man and they step into the crowded room. White Christmas lights are strung up over the bar and all along the walls. The soft glow has a way of muting shadows. Inside an eclectic bunch of nomads, exiles, and transients. This place is a road delta, where all the road people are gathered to be drug through fertile mud and pushed out into the rough ocean of night. Every one is gliding, swimming, floating, flying through the bar in this uncanny white light. They are hanging in air on the strings of blown-out speakers defiantly proclaiming "Sweet dreams are made of this," sung by an old worn-out woman clutching a microphone with white knuckles. Her head is sagging a little and she is shaking to the beat in a kind of erotic convulsion.

Samuel pushes the young man from behind toward the bar. Samuel is beaming, exchanging nods and pinches as he moves through the dense crowd.

When they belly up to the bar, Samuel waves his hand and yells at the plump Latina bartender and she sashays toward them.

-Chicken fingers!

Samuel's yell is a high-pitched warble.

-Two buds and two ta-kill-yas! *Arhrraaooooooo!*

A donkey noise maybe, or a cow noise.

I stumble two feet from my door and fall on the concrete. I lie there for a moment. Breathing. Head spinning. At this moment I can feel the sun breaking over the rooftops. Sunlight is warming my back. I could sleep here on the ground. I could roll over into the street and quietly wait until I am run over by someone on their way to Wall Street, just a bump on a sunny morning drive through the city.

I could get up. And go inside.

Both my palms are scuffed and bleeding from my fall. The left is worse. How am I going to masturbate?

-Fuck.

I get up using the sides of my hands and step to my door. I fumble with the key in the lock. The door is open and I step inside. The sun is already warming my room. I kick off my shoes and wash my hands in the sink. A few bits of gravel are left on a plate I used for toast a week ago.

When I turn around I see my room. My little life. I see my unread books, my unslept-on bed, my unworked-on desk, my hand-me-down clothes scattered about, and my coffee table, filled with unfinished drawings of a woman I have seen only once. Now twice.

Among these drawings is a single painting. I don't even remember the act of painting it. I think I painted it a couple of weeks ago, but the last few weeks are a daze. The painting is small, an unfolding sprig of green leaves, opening to reveal a disembodied red aorta, floating in its center like a young rose bud.

The painting looks like death. I gather up the stacks of paper. Months of hermitic ravings. I pile them neatly and put them inside a plastic Food Emporium bag. There are a lot of them, almost a hundred, each page uncompleted.

140

-Why is it that something formed so perfectly in my imagination fails so harshly when I try to put it to the page?

No one answers. There is only a rare New York City silence and I am actually listening for something. When I realize it I am ashamed. I realize I have built an entire world, in my mind, with Emile. We were going to save each other from this place, from—something, I don't know. I have been dreaming about a life with a phantom. She has just been living her life like I never existed. I am alone. I am alone and I have no idea how I am going to survive this.

I place the bag on the coffee table and begin to take my clothes off. My hands are tender, so I use my fingertips. Button button button button. My clothes are so worn through, I expect them to disintegrate when they hit the floor.

Getting down on my hands and knees I reach under the bed and pull out my mirror. I prop it up on the bed and I sit on the floor in front of it. I look for my schizophrenic pixie-haired mother. I look for my sad-eyed and bearded father. I want to see their reflection in the mirror so I can throw a fist through it. They have taunted me in this reflection before. They have pushed and prodded at me. I have followed them through this glass window and walked the land that stripped them of their sanity and their life. I am looking into the mirror for some sign, for some signal.

What I see is a man sitting naked and alone on the floor. Flaccid penis. Half a dozen claw marks on his chest and neck. His left cheek is swollen from a girl, whose name he doesn't know, who caught him with a balled fist in the face the night before.

The figure in the mirror is threadbare. Permeable. Transparent. Empty. I don't like

141

what I see.

I stand up. I take a shower and put different clothes on. I gather up the drawings and the single painting and stack them in a pile atop my full-length mirror. I walk out my door to the street corner. There is a green steel trash can there. I walk up to it and stop. Rather than throw them all away, I set just them on the ground in a pile next to the can.

I go back inside my apartment and start packing my things into plastic bags. It is time for me to go. Home.

"Baby, babe, I'm gonna leave you!" Samuel's voice is crystal. Glassy-eyed and sick, the young man takes it all in. The Office is a brimming mass. A woman with impossibly large breasts is dancing a few feet in front of Samuel. Her heavy rocking and Samuel's serenade have captured the whole bar. A few hands are in the air and there is even a lighter out, swaying at arm's length to the rhythm.

The young man watches the flame struggle, a tiny thing drinking oxygen. The sputtering, choking dance is keeping perfect rhythm to "leave you in the summer time."

The young man's mouth is slightly agape. He is thinking it is a beautiful little flame. It shines like a disembodied star in the milky glow of a hypnotized and drunk bar. "I can hear it calling me back home."

He slides off his barstool. He pitches to the side and is lifted up by an anonymous and encouraging hand. He could step inside that tiny flame and be transported. "Baby, ohhh! Don't you hear it calling?"

There is a chorus forming, because everyone knows the words to this one: "Baby, we're gonna go walking through the park everyday."

And the young man feels his voice join in the song. It is all in place, the helping hand, the solitary flame, the breasts so impossible and Samuel crooning at the microphone with one hand supporting his tightened belly and the other holding the microphone close to his lips: "But now I have to go away. Baaaby, baaaby *breeeeeeeeeeeeeeeeeeeeeeeeehhhhhk.*"

Samuel screeches into the microphone like a dying rabbit. His dying animal noise is underscored by Led Zeppelin, coming to climax through busted speakers. There is a collective lurch followed by a silence so oppressive even Jimmy Page can't cut through the line.

143

The drunken young man bursts into laughter.
It starts in his belly and wiggles hysterically
up to his eyebrows.

-Youu diid iit!

It's all he can get out between laughter and
gasps, but it is enough to bring a straight
white smile out of Samuel's bearded mouth.

-Get the fuck outta here you barnyard freak!
a big trucker yells, waving his fist at Samuel.

The enormous breasts vanish into the crowd at
the sight of the balled fist. There is no flame
and the music has shuffled forward to an old
country song. The bartender is standing with
her arms crossed, shaking her head at Samuel.

The magic is gone and the young man cannot
stop laughing. He is doubled over, tears in his
eyes. He tries to stop, but when Samuel grabs
him by the arm and begins to pull him out of
the bar he starts laughing again, even more
passionately than before. Laughter. It hurts
him and it won't stop. Bent half over with his
feet dragging over the gravel, the young man's
laughter grows into something hysterical. The
laughter turns into a cough, and while he's
being tugged along by the arm, the coughing
turns into a spray of vomit.

-Oh, Shit.

Samuel is high-stepping away as the young
man leans into the wheel well of a big rig and
dumps a big load of tequila and chicken fingers
onto the lug nuts of an eighteen-wheeler.

-Come on, now. Puke and rally! Come on,
Tommy.

The young man wipes his mouth and looks up at
the portly trucker.

-You called me Tomm—*aruungh.*

Only a dry heave this time. He wipes the

144

tears from his eyes with the forearm of his
shirt. He smiles.

—Man, that felt good. I haven't laughed, or
sang, or even puked in ages. Thanks, Samuel.
Sorry we got kicked outta there.

—Aw fuck 'em. Now that was a rabbit noise!

They stumble over to the side of Samuel's
truck, leaning against the trailer and catching
their breaths. Samuel turns to unzip his fly and
commences drawing the rough shape of bunny ears
in piss on the dirt.

The young man follows suit and begins to let
out a long stream when he stumbles again and
sprays a line over Sam's right boot.

—Jesus!

Samuel turns to the young man and pisses
out what's left on the leg of the young man's
jeans. Both men run out of fluid and stand there
for a moment, peckers in hand, before they
burst into laughter again.

—I can't stop! the young man gasps.

He is trying to stifle the laugh when a
hard blow lands on the side of his temple.
Down in an instant, he is lying on the ground
in a muddy puddle of his own piss. There is
some yelling about faggots and freaks and
cocksuckers. He hears only a scared yelp from
Samuel before another blow lands just above
the back of his neck. His head pitches forward
sending his mouth down into wet gravel. He is
kicked once more in his ribs. He struggles to
stand up, but then there is only the roaring of
a truck engine and more yelling and spinning
tires and the air is filled in a cloud of dust.

When the dust settles, the parking lot is
empty again, save for the young man on the
ground. The men have returned to the bar.
Samuel's truck is gone. The music from The

Office is pouring into the empty lot.

The young man gets up, dusts himself uselessly, and starts walking back toward the road. He walks until the sound of crickets begins to muffle the karaoke bar. He walks until all there is the sound of crickets and highway noise. The air grows more dense he walks the few miles north toward Erie Lake and the Canadian expanse beyond.

By noon I am tossing the last of my books and clothes into a small moving truck. I only have enough stuff to fill maybe a third of the truck. When I first moved to New York I had two duffel bags and a plant. The plant died while I was in college, so other than an accumulation of books and a few pieces of furniture I rescued from the trash, I don't possess anything of much value. A van would have been plenty big enough, but I found out this morning they don't let you take vans out of the city.

In spite of my few possessions, I have left quite a bit behind. My bed is leaning against a street-side light pole. My few plates and kitchen things are stacked neatly on the curb. I even washed them and they will make a nice addition to someone's street-salvaged apartment. The street is, after all, where I found all of these things.

The city seems to breed this. Nothing you can carry will bring the city with you when you leave. So why take anything? People dump their lives in piles on street corners and in the morning everyone, rich or poor, picks through the remains and takes back what's needed. I know rich people do this too. They just collect earlier. You can only find Brooks Brothers or Williams and Sonoma just after daybreak. By 10:00 a.m. the good stuff is all gone.

I also talked to my landlord this morning. He agreed to give me back my security deposit if I vacuumed. I pulled the vacuum from the hallway closet and when I tried to turn it on the dust bag exploded into a cloud. So I left the vacuum there with my keys on the sink.

I look over the meager contents of the apartment I have packed into a tiny corner in the back of the truck. I pull down the door and walk around to the cab. There is a huge picture of a monarch butterfly, floating over a U-Haul logo. Monarchs migrate through Nebraska every

147

fall. Maybe this summer the Great Plains will
be fluttering with those black speckled wings.
Butterflies in the afternoon and cicadas in the
evenings. I am not exactly excited to go home,
but I am feeling something like a hunger to
return there. I want to smell the air that I
smelled as a child. I have lost something since
I moved to this city, something essential.
I don't know what it is, but perhaps I will
be able to catch a whiff of it in the air in
Nebraska.

Without looking back at my apartment, I am
lifting myself into the cab, turning the engine
over and pulling out onto the street. The truck
has a full tank of gas and there is something
powerful about that. The road is waiting for
me. It doesn't care if I have not called my job
yet to tell them I won't be coming in tonight.
Or tomorrow. It doesn't care that I haven't
called Frank to say good-bye. The road sits
patiently stretching out to the west, ready to
receive me on my journey.

I pull out onto Knickerbocker. I drive past
the Mexican and Puerto Rican diners and bars.
I drive past the lofts of transplanted white
suburbanites who, like me, have found their way
to Brooklyn. I drive past Frank's place, into
Williamsburg and over the bridge where the sign
reads:

LEAVING BROOKLYN OY VEY

As soon as I hit Manhattan the traffic
bottlenecks. To make it across town, up the
Henry Hudson, and over the Washington Bridge
will take me a couple hours. Even still, if
I drive hard on I-80 I know I can make it to
Omaha by tomorrow night. Omaha. There is no
reason to go back home. What's left of my
family has moved to Phoenix, all my friends

have moved away, my sister Hollie is living in Milwaukee. I could drive straight across the country to LA, where at least some of my friends from college have moved, but the idea makes me nauseous.

-Omaha or bust.

I honk my horn at nothing and nothing but the chaos of Delancey Street responds. I am at ease behind the wheel. I turn up First Avenue and shoot for Fourteenth St. to cut across town. Out of the window of my U-Haul the city looks spectacular and totally indifferent. There are rows of majestic buildings and throngs of people who can't be bothered to notice me make my escape. I am being pumped through a sluggish clogged artery, past busy organs and tissues that have no concern for anything that functions to serve them directly.

I turn left on Fourteenth and start cutting across town. Traffic bottlenecks again at Union Square. There is some performance or film production taking place on an island sidewalk amid the throng of cars and people. There is a little white circus tent with lights and cables strewn every which way.

It looks interesting and I consider pulling over, double-parking, and taking a look. The road is calling me out of the city, though, so I give the brightly lit tent a last glance over my shoulder and turn my attention back to the traffic. The West Side Highway is only a few avenues away and then it is a straight shot to the George Washington Bridge and then I'm out.

On Sixth Avenue I am stopped at a red and across the street I see a bike messenger collide with a pedestrian. The pedestrian is a tall blonde with knee-high leather boots. She is sprawled out on the ground, stunned, with a queer look of disbelief on her face. The cars lurch forward past her. A few people

149

are stepping around her and the messenger is hurriedly getting back on his bicycle. I could stop and get out and help her, but I don't. There are people everywhere and I am already being pumped through the intersection.

I am making better time than I thought, and the Hudson River appears and guides me up the highway. On my left is New Jersey, looking gray even in the afternoon sun. To my right, Manhattan rises up looking Technicolor in spite of being brick and concrete.

I could turn around and go back to my apartment. I could crash at Frank's for a while and just try to pull it together. Start fresh. I have almost a grand in my bank account, which is only because I haven't been drinking every night for the last couple months. But it would be enough to sit on for a month. I could get a new job. I could get involved again.

I see the George Washington Bridge. The highway twists under an aqueduct, slides past the tenements of West Harlem, and feeds me onto the bridge.

I am on the upper roadway with a mighty view of the Hudson. There are a surprising number of trees here. Pennsylvania looks like Pennsylvania. I am driving into that. I look in my rearview and the city is a sprawl behind me, calling me back.

I cross to the other side of the river. The highway looks like highway. I am traveling west on I-80. I light up a cigarette and don't look back.

He steps off the road onto a gravelly shore.
Lake Erie is vast. His boots sink a little into
the mud as he walks toward the water. Vomiting
and a couple blows to the head have sobered him
up quickly and the air that hits his lungs is
crisp and vital. Across the water, the lights
of a Canadian industrial complex shine with
sterility. The lights are dim and almost hidden
by the distance. There are a few small towns
on the outskirts of the industrial center, but
they are all but shrouded completely in a thick
mist.

This anonymous piece of shoreline is the end
of this small bit of America. A boundary line.
On the other side there is something new and
different. He could swim, maybe, but he knows
there'd be no chance of making it. There are
miles and miles of water between the shores.
There are no boats around. On the American side
there are no lakeside cottages or industrial
ports. He could walk around the edge of the
water and find some small town, offering passage
to Canada and a new life. But there is no port
town in sight. He could walk all day and find
nothing. He has no money for passage. He has no
passport. He has nowhere to go.

He had hoped Samuel would cut back and pick
him up. They could go to Maine together and he
could learn to catch lobsters and live off the
land. His hands would harden up from working
with rope and wood. He could do that.

But Samuel just got back on the road. The
young man understood. Roads take you somewhere
and Samuel had somewhere to go. Maine would
have been nice, though. He had never been to
Maine. He had never even eaten lobster. He
probably wouldn't have liked it anyway.

This is it, then. He looks out across
the choppy murk. The water doesn't smell
particularly inviting so there is no sense in

cleaning himself up in it. At this point it would be hard to catch another ride. He can smell his own ripeness exacerbated by dried piss. He smells and looks like a vagrant.

There is no bike. His motorcycle might still be sitting there waiting for him to return with a red can full of gas. Then he and his little green bike could be on their way. They would drive, held in the spell of the road forever. But the bike is gone. There is no going back.

This is it. Muddy boots. A big lake. Canada inviting and almost within reach. If something could just reach out and push him to the other side.

But nothing does. Highway noise and crickets. Driftwood and pebbles lapping against the shore in an infinite cycle. He is a little piece of drift wood. He sighs and turns away from the water. He walks in his own footprints back to the road.

He is walking down the little utility road he and Samuel came in on off the turnpike. Suddenly he feels afraid for the first time since he left his home. He knew the destination of this trip, but he didn't know how to get there or where it was. He stands there for a moment with light gray mud caked to his boots. Crickets and highway noise. He will walk back to the turnpike. He could walk a little farther still.

The road is lined with the dark silhouettes of swaying trees. Green streetlights stretch out intermittently pouring sentinel pools of milky light water onto the asphalt. He can see the lights hanging atop black poles in the distance like lanterns. As he approaches the first streetlight the road begins to materialize. Though the road is smooth, when illuminated, it has a rough appearance. A million tiny shadows cast in the infinitesimal canyon land of the poured concrete.

Once he passes under the center of the light his shadow begins to stretch out before him and he imagines he is a lone giant, marching across a desolate universe in search of his lost mate. His shadow grows with each footstep and at the same time it begins to disintegrate until it is lost again in the shadow.

The moon has betrayed him and left him alone to walk under the dim light of the stars. He can probably find the moon somewhere if he stares long enough. A new moon is masked in shadow but it is there, hiding in the black sky. The moon's shadow is what he feels projected upon him. The shadow is oppressive and makes the stars more dim and the darkness of the sparse woods more dense.

He is grateful to the road for being there to guide him. Most of the warmth it collected from the sun is gone, but still it is a comfort. The road is solid and unwavering. He thinks if he had to walk through unmarked woods, following only the moan of the highway noise carried on the wind, he would never come through them. The road is sure of itself. And though no one is here to share in his journey, the road was made by a brotherhood of men and women. Their hands carved the way through these woods and it will lead him back to the turnpike. People were here and they left him this sign to point the way. The road is his witness, his companion.

He doesn't sing or talk. He is focused ahead. He can walk through till morning. When it is light again, he will know where he is and can decide what to do.

He is hungry, but he doesn't pay any attention to the whining of his stomach. The muscles in his legs coil and retract in a smooth rhythm. His hands are tucked into his jacket pockets and his head is poised atop his neck. He is purposeful, with intent. He has somewhere to go and doesn't give a damn how long it takes to walk there. He is on his way.

It is midnight. I am exhausted. The road is rolling rolling rolling endlessly beneath me and I keep thinking of the subway. It had a way of putting me to sleep. I always woke up, just before my stop. The road has the same effect, but if I fall asleep, I will end up smashing into a tree or rolling this truck into a ditch.

I keep craning my neck to look upward through the windshield. There is no moon in the sky and the stars are utterly brilliant. For years I have only looked at the stars through the jealous veil of the city lights, piss poor compared to this night sky. I cannot remember when I last saw stars this beautiful.

I have memories of campfires and the reflection of stars in mountain glacier lakes. There are memories of pulling off to the side of a country road to pee only to be awestruck and transfixed under the Midwestern night sky. I can't remember the last time I'd seen stars like this. Clearly it has been too long.

I am suddenly relieved to be here, in this moment. I did not have any idea a day ago that I would be here, under these stars, and for the first time everything feels right. As soon as that feeling settles in me I realize I must call Frank. A heart pang strikes my chest. I did not mean to hurt him and he will be in a panic if he finds out I am gone. He might think I am dead or something.

At the next exit I will grab some coffee and take a piss and call Frank. That's good. I feel better already. I can apologize for the way I acted at Dumont and for my disappearing act. He will totally understand and be glad I called. He will tell me I am crazy as usual and to turn my ass around and come back to the city. I can crash with him for a while and get a new place. It'll be good.

A sigh pours out of me. I crane my neck again

155

for another look at these awesome stars. They are so bright. A new moon for a new beginning. I almost grin when I see an exit sign marking gas and food.

-Gas, coffee, piss, call Frank, go home.

He sees the lights of the turnpike in the reflection of a dark mirror. He is drinking water out of the sink of a roadside gas station. The station is closed, but the bathroom is attached to a small storage building and the door has been left open. The lights do not work, so he has the door propped open with his foot.

He is grateful for the darkness; the idea of seeing a clear picture of his face is horrifying. It has been several days on the road without a shave and he can feel stubble beginning to thicken on his face. He has not worn a beard for several years. He had started growing a beard when his wife was committed to a mental hospital. She was hospitalized for two years and his beard had become long and shaggy.

He remembers shaving one morning when he came home from the hospital. He had been wearing a beard and that particular morning the doctors, a lawyer, and his family had gathered to tell him that he needed to divorce his wife. They told him that she was sick, that she would never be the same woman he married. They told him he would go into tens of thousands of dollars of debt if he didn't divorce her.

He said he wanted to see her one more time. At first they said no, but he had pressed, saying he would sign nothing until he was able to see her one last time. The doctors led him to a white room, enclosed in glass windows. They made him look at her from outside the room, though the windows. They said she was sleeping. She was sedated and her head had been shaved. They had given her shock treatment and had her doped up on god knows what. Her face was slack and her eyes were open but vacant. He tapped on the glass, but she did not respond.

It was then that he decided to take her with him. He thought he could feel her stepping into his body. Imagining her hand in his, he signed the papers terminating their marriage and his legal responsibility for her. He could feel her presence when he left the hospital. He could feel her in the car with him as he drove home. He thought if he shaved she would be able to recognize his face better and as he stared in the mirror he could almost feel her, looking through his eyes at his reflection.

He had been growing the beard since she first went to the hospital. It was hanging off his face. A few early strands of gray had begun to show, intermingling in the dark brown curls around his chin. He could feel her presence, the love of his life, the mother of his children. Together they lathered up his face and slowly cut through the dense beard. They didn't cut his face or even leave razor burn. It was gentle. Together they rinsed the last bits of foam away. Together they looked at his clean-shaven face and he thought he looked handsome. He almost smiled. He reached out to touch his face and when his fingers touched the glass, she vanished. The spell was broken. He was alone in his house. His daughter and son were staying at his mother's. He looked at his reflection and he just saw himself standing there with his arm outstretched.

blood knot

troubled hedgerows

pinioned by light

you lost

me

Again he is alone, standing in the unlit bathroom of an empty roadside gas station. His son and daughter are sleeping in warm beds at their grandmother's. In the mirror he can only see his dark shape silhouetted by the lights of a not-too-distant turnpike.

"Hello, this is Frank. Please leave a message."

There is a beep. I am shocked and annoyed. There is a pause.

-Hi. Frank. It's me. I…

My voice gets caught in my throat. I cough into the phone.

-Frank, sorry. I am gone. I wanted to let you know. Don't worry about me. I mean, I'm fine. Hey I didn't expect your machine… I just wanted to tell you I—

"You have eight more seconds after the beep. If you are finished please hang up. For other options, please press five."

-OK, I am out of time. Frank. Hey man, I am going to Omaha. I can call when—

Beep.

-Christ. Fuck. OK, that was stupid.

I try to press five and I press six instead. The phone beeps again, then hangs up and I am listening to a dial tone.

-Fucking fuckin fuckn *fuck*.

I slam the phone down.

-That's why I don't have a cell phone! Assholes.

The gas station attendant is giving me a disapproving look, like we are in a library or something. I just throw my hand into the air, grab my coffee, and head back out to the truck.

I start it up and pull out toward the on-ramp. There is a sign, which reads LEFT FOR I-80 EAST, RIGHT FOR I-80 WEST. I wait there a moment, with the truck idling. I am wide awake after that episode. I can make it back to New York by the morning or make it across Pennsylvania.

If I were Frank, I could call my parents and ask them what to do. Frank's mother is a gun-toting Texan angel who sends him care packages full of socks and underwear. My mother burned all of my toys after a Christmas visit when I was 8 or 9. She was jealous of all the attention and presents we got. That was another trip back to the hospital for her.

I could track my mother down and ask her what I should do with my life. That's a funny thought. She would talk about her life instead. She always does. Blood knots and white light, hedgerows and lidless eyes. She tells wild stories and I can never decide what is true and what is crazy make-believe. No. I am on my own. I always have been and I always will be.

I am frustrated, but I am activated. I start to chew the inside of my lower lip. I step on the gas and turn right. West on I-80.

The bathroom door closes behind him. There is another green light hanging over the gas station. At the base of the light pole is a pay phone. He walks past the pumps up to the phone. He doesn't need to look to know there is no change in his pockets. He picks up the phone and listens to the dial tone. He listens until the phone begins to give the off-the-hook warning, then he hangs up the phone and stands there for a moment.

Who can he call? His mother? His sister? A gust of wind hits him. There was no breeze before, but there seems to be something blowing up from the south. It has gotten chilly and is starting to get late.

He picks up the phone again and presses zero, but before the operator's voice can say hello he hangs up again. He shakes his head.

-Stupid.

There is a swarm of moths bombarding the green light above him. He looks up at them, tapping against the glass lamp, all in a bustle to get a little closer to the promising green light.

In the distance the lights on the turnpike are a whitish yellow. Even from far off he can tell that the lights are much higher off the ground and much brighter. It is hard to tell what time it is. The sky is turning a purplish hue. He has walked through the night.

It's hard for him to walk away from the phone. All he has to do is reach out and make a call and someone will come to get him. He forces his mind not to linger on the idea of home. His eyes focus on the details of the phone itself. He wonders where the phone was made. Who made it? Plastic injection molds on an assembly line somewhere in a southern town, making hundreds of phones in a day. Maybe thousands.

He rubs his hands together and turns away from the pay phone. How far? he wonders. The turnpike looks close, but it could still be a mile or two. Easy walk. It felt good washing out his mouth and cleaning his face in the dark bathroom. His muscles cool back down quickly though, and as he starts walking his legs are kinky and stiff. His feet are holding up well in his hand-me-down boots. He did not notice the mud caking his boots in the bathroom and didn't think to clean them before heading out again. He walks back toward the utility road with muddied gray boots.

The road winds a circuitous route to the turnpike. It would probably be quicker to cut straight across through the high grass between the gas station and the interstate. He furrows his brow at this. No. Stay on the road. The road will take you there in good time. He is not afraid of this. There is no hurry. He has come a long way and seen many beautiful things.

I am afraid. I am afraid to live. I am damaged goods. The road is wearing me down again. It is very late. Only a few of the brightest stars are still in the sky. They have been with me all night. No radio, no more phone calls. Just immersive brilliant acupuncture in light, hanging above me, seeping in through the windshield

I am running like hell from myself. Who wouldn't? I realize I am truly horrified. I can only manage contact with a woman if it is filthy and heartless. The second someone gets close I am reduced to a jelly.

I want to blame my mother. She keeps intruding on my thoughts. She used to joke with me about being stoned when I was born. She hadn't even smoked cigarettes while carrying my sister. She would almost brag about dragging my sister to her drug dealer while I was still in her belly, a little invader. She spent the last trimester of my growth stoned on anything she could get her hands on. After I was born, she just let go completely. When I was a little older, on visits, she would tease me about this. She has all sorts of jokes about me. She says when I was born, the doctor handed her a roll of toilet paper. I smile. She is really quite funny, my mother.

I don't feel crazy or insane, but I am scared I might be. Where do you run when you are trying to escape from yourself? I thought Emile could be someone one who could save me. I was afraid that if I told her who I was and how much damage I was capable of doing, she would leave. But she was never real in the first place. I fell completely in love and was heartbroken by someone who didn't even know I existed.

I thought leaving New York City would heal me. I thought I would come out of it OK. I thought I was going to be fine. I realize how

hard I have worked to protect myself from
falling in love. I fall in love anyway. I
chase love like a heroine addict. Senseless
slobbering bastard.

-I hate myself.

Fuck, it hurts to say it out loud. I am so
angry at myself. I bite down on my lower lip.
The stars are trembling through my clouded
eyes. Tears. I am crying.

-This is so stupid.

I just want to be home. I just want to go
to my grandmother's old house and lie on her
carpet.

I take a deep breath and let it slowly hiss
out of my pursed lips. I wipe my eyes and look
up at the sky. Only a few stars left. They are
twinkling now, one by one. That moon never
showed its crooked face. A new moon to fall
for.

I swallow the last of my coffee, which has
grown cold. At some point I am going to cross a
time zone. Chicago. I won't get that far until
around noon. For some reason I can't decide
whether crossing the time zone means it will be
an hour earlier or later. Earlier, I think.

It is late and I am tired, but I think I'm
going to get an extra hour of daylight when
I cross the time zone. I can drive straight
through. Like my father did.

The turnpike is a wide four-lane boulevard separated by an island of trimmed grass. Patchy clouds, holding rain, have started to fill what was left of the night sky. It has already sprinkled once, but it didn't last. The rain has left a greasy sheen on the road.

He steps off the on-ramp, onto the shoulder of the big road. The concrete of the turnpike feels different through the soles of his boots than the asphalt of the utility road. The concrete is dense, but the ground feels almost hollow beneath it, like there is a subterranean city buried under the road. He takes a few steps onto the highway, then stops to give his legs a shake. His muscles are tired and tight and threatening to cramp. He is on the north side of the turnpike and the traffic is pointed west, so he heads west.

The sun will be coming up at his back in an hour or so. The sky is already beginning to blend into softer hues, the color of new bruises. He begins walking and he feels he is close.

He walks. The western horizon is still dark and disappears out of his sight. There will be a lot of interchanges and overpasses along this big road. Commercial gas stations, diners, adult supercenters. Lake Erie is a sliver of black void to his right. He is too far away to see the Canadian lights on the other side of the lake now. There is only the dark horizon ahead and spools of color rolling out from the approaching dawn behind him.

A few cars and trucks whiz by. He pays the cars no mind. There is very little chance anyone will stop for him now. No one stops for hitchhikers on the big interstates. Hitchhikers are dangerous. He could stroll along walking backward with his thumb outstretched for miles and no one would stop. Not even the truckers.

This interstate is for people who have somewhere to go. Eighty miles an hour, they jettison past without even a blink of brake lights.

He is not looking for a ride. He wouldn't know what to do if someone stopped. He would probably walk wordlessly right past them. Or maybe not. He could catch a ride. At eighty miles an hour, he could be back home in the late evening on this road. On this road the distance that took days on back highways on his old bike he could pummel in twelve hours.

He never liked interstate travel, too impersonal. The roadside communities are full of young people who just feel betrayed to be born in such a shitty place. Nothing like being born in New York, or Chicago, or San Diego. Even growing up on a farm is better, because there is at least a sense of place.

If you were brought up along the interstate and everyone you met in your whole life had come and gone in ten minutes with a full tank of gas and a bag of chips, there would be no chance of escape or hope. How would you learn to touch someone? How would you learn to connect?

That is what he didn't like about these roads. All it took was an extra lane on the highway for America to annihilate the connection of one small community to the next. You could roll ten battalions of troops anywhere in this country in two straight days of driving. Tanks could roll from one ocean to the other in under a week. And even if they never do, they could, and that's what matters.

This road is clinically perfect. No contact. No touch. Just walking over a lost subterranean city, in muddied boots, with hands buried in pockets. A bit of rain starts to fall again. The drops are cold pellets, but they feel good.

Bracing. He raises his head and continues to walk, leaving tiny droplets of mud on the road behind him. Pieces of footprints that are already starting to wash away.

Stroudsburg. Berwick. Milton. Lock Haven. Snow Shoe. Clearfield. DuBois. Clarion. Grove City.

Sentinels along the gauntlet. Little towns that mean nothing to me. Exits. North. South. Turn around, go east. Go east!

EAT. ADULT. GAS. CAMPERS. FARM EQUIPMENT. CHRIST SAVES!!!

Glowing green signs. I can't think of the word. It is reflective, but something else. These signs. These names. Huge Neon everything. BIG BOY. Dinosaurs. Huge ceramic hot dogs.

I cannot decipher this madness. I am exhausted. I stopped at a travel plaza for coffee and gas again an hour ago. There was a condom machine in the bathroom with the drawing of a ridiculously busty blonde. In bed she would kill me. Maim me. Use my shattered bones to carve a notch into her black policewoman's belt. And she wants me to buy a condom. Horrified, I bolted back to my truck. I hadn't paid and the cashier thought I was going to run for it.

-You forgot your coffee. Hey! You have to pay for that gas!

The incredulous look I threw at her demanded silence. Wild-eyed and dignified I walked up and threw forty bucks on the counter.

-Keep the *change*!

In the truck I can only shake my head. That was stupid. What is she, a cabbie? The coffee is long gone and I am trying to decide why my mouth feels the way it does. I have smoked copious numbers of cigarettes and it feels like my teeth are floating. My incisors, my eyeteeth, my molars, my floating wisdom teeth are all exposed nerve endings and I am sure they will fall out. Perfect. Bald and toothless in my twenties.

Droplets of rain start to hit the windshield. I roll down my window and cold air blows into the cab. The breeze is good to wake me up, but the wind is too chilly and the noise is loud so I roll the window back up.

There are a few rain clouds in the sky, but nothing serious. The sun will probably burn them off. I look in my rearview and, sure enough, the sky is starting to change colors. Dawn is a way off yet, but soon. I am glad I am not driving east. I don't have sunglasses and I think the morning sun would melt the eyes out of my head.

Another road sign approaches fast, like a disembodied glowing ghoul.

WELCOME TO OHIO

SO MUCH TO DISCOVER!

Ohio? O-hi-o. Fuck yeah. I think that is halfway. I don't know anybody in Ohio. Not a soul. If I did I might stop and crash on their couch. That might be awkward, I don't know. It doesn't matter.

I should pull over and sleep. I am not nodding off yet, but my eyes are heavy and I am feeling vague and delirious. I think the most alive part of my body is my mouth. My tongue is a piece of dry leather and the roof of my mouth is throbbing. It feels like I need a cigarette really bad, but that doesn't make sense. I might puke if I smoke again. That might wake me up.

I pull out a cigarette. I decide my dad was nuts. What sort of weird machine just drives like this forever? He was good at driving, though. Toward the end of his life, when he could no longer get work as a woodworker, he became a truck driver. He would be on the road for two or three weeks at a time. It was like he never slept on the road because when he came home he would sleep like a bear on the coach in my grandmother's living room or on the floor of her study.

The last time I saw him I woke in the middle of the night and went upstairs. He did not like to be disturbed in the night and I had never gone into the study while he was sleeping before. That night I just woke up, tiptoed upstairs, and lay down next to him. I tried very hard not to wake him, I just laid very still with my eyes open, listening to him breathe. I was startled when he whispered to me,

-Are you OK?

-Yes, I whispered back.

He put his hand on my shoulder and squeezed me softly and nothing more was said. When I woke up he was gone. I had slept through the night and waking up on the carpet of my grandmother's study made me think of camping. My sister and I just assumed he had gone back on the road. He hadn't said good-bye, but it was not unusual for him to leave in the middle of the night so he could get an early start.

We learned later that he had in fact gone up north to look for a job as a woodworker or in a machine shop. He didn't have money for a train ride back home. I remember waking up happy and stupid and skipping up the stairs of my grandmother's house. I was surprised to see my whole family sitting in the living room. I knew immediately something was wrong. My aunt told me that was my daddy was gone. They said he was hitchhiking home and was hit by a car. A hit-and-run. That is what we were told as children, anyway.

Ohio. Halfway. I turn the radio on, but there is nothing catchy playing and the noise hurts my teeth. I pull a cigarette out of my pocket and light it up. After one drag, I gag

171

and change my mind. I am about to toss it out the window when I see an old bum with his thumb out. I don't see him until I am almost on top of him and then he is gone in a blur.

His face flashed in my headlight for just a moment. I could see him start to wince from my headlights and then he was gone. He was wearing a faded army jacket and his eyes were black pits. I look in my rearview and he is already a tiny gray shape vanishing on the road.

-Crazy old bastard.

I raise the cigarette back to my mumbling lips. I am glad I didn't toss it out the window. That old bum kinda freaked me out and I want to smoke.

There is a sparse exit ramp and an overpass with a sign that says there is a town eight miles north. He hikes up the on-ramp and onto the overpass. He is awake and his mind is sharp. On the overpass a car slows and from a rolled-down window a portly bald man with wide blue suspenders offers him a ride into town.

He politely declines and the car drives away. He thinks, *Here I am*. Just so, he stands on the overpass and waits. There is a small walkway on the overpass and something like a ledge to sit on. The sky is light, but the sun has not yet crested the horizon.

It is nice to be a bit higher up. As if being twenty or so feet off the ground gives you a better view of the sun cresting the surface of the earth. It does, he thinks. It does. So he waits for the sun on the ledge, like he is in the grandstand of a baseball stadium.

His chest rises and falls with his breath. He can feel blood coursing through his legs. His feet are hot and wet with sweat. He pulls a silver ring from his pocket and slips it over his ring finger. The simple turquoise stones on the ring look like tiny pieces of sky. He runs his palm across the smooth concrete. *Someone built this*, he thinks. Someone's hands may have run across this very surface, proud that the line ran straight and true. He can almost feel that hand. Or maybe the concrete remembers its touch and has been waiting all these years for the warm hand to return. He feels welcomed.

The sun. First a sliver, then two cusps. The sky above it has more colors than there are words for. A slice, then a half. His breath has slowed. The sun is moving so fast. He can stare at it and see it racing skyward. He wants the sun to stop, to remain suspended in that perfect moment, but it keeps coming. He grips the concrete ledge to brace himself against the dizzying coriolis. The earth spins against the oncoming sun. It is a naked orb. Brilliant. It is right in front of him, in plain sight. The sun bores into his eyes. It is an inferno impossible to truly see.

His breath stops for a moment and he closes his eyes. *I have seen so much*, he thinks. It comes to him in a kaleidoscope of images. Not memories, but shapes and shades. Skin, sunlit hair, shadows, tiny hands, rough-hewn wood, colored glass hanging in the window, whispers, dishes, epic water, dreams, flight.

He can feel everything he is touching, every pore feels fabric and skin and concrete and wind and sunlight pouring in. There is so much fullness.

The truck vibrates and howls as I float onto the deep grooves of the shoulder.

I jerk awake.

-Christ!

I shake my head and wipe my eyes. OK. I am falling asleep at the wheel. It is time for a break. I crack the window and the cool air again cuts across my face. I shift in my seat, roll my shoulders, and run my tongue over my teeth.

I feel better. More awake. That was close. I can't believe I did that. I yawn with a huge open mouth. That was a nap, at least. I smile. Power nap. Seven seconds, good to go.

-No reason to be alarmed, ladies and gentlemen. The kid's gonna make it.

I only have two cigarettes left and the tank is almost empty. Fifty miles. Fifty miles and I will stop. Plenty of gas for that and I can take a walk.

There is a sign for an exit in two miles. OK. Two miles. That is better. I will get some coffee and smokes and shake it off. Driving is when you find out what being addicted to cigarettes means. That and cancer, I guess. Another big sign, saying, HEY STUPID, YOU SHOULD HAVE QUIT.

On my right I can see a strip of Lake Erie reflecting golden sunlight. It looks like the golden sword of a titan, lying forgotten on the side of the road. I can check out a bit of the sunrise in my rearview. The Sun is almost clear of the horizon.

It's going to be a beautiful day. The air coming in through the window doesn't feel quite as cold as it did.

Another sign for the exit is coming up. One mile. Then immediately behind it another sign has a picture of a gas tank on it with an arrow that points north and says 8 MILES. I can see the exit and the overpass rolling up, but there is no town in sight, or even a building.

-Aw shit. Screw that.

OK. Fifty miles. Fifty miles with the sun at my back and the wind in my face. Easy.

He looks out in a moment that stretches across centuries. He comes out of time. He sees the sun swell in its final moment. He watches as it implodes. A supernova breaks through the clouds and cuts rake-like lines across the misty horizon. The earth is still, a quiet communion.

The hollow sound of the wind becomes muted, as if very far off. He sees it all and feels perfect serenity. He can feel his blood moving. Each of his bones supports his body against the weight of gravity. The overpass sways beneath him. It lasts only a moment. A white rental truck is bustling down the road toward him. He takes a breath, then holds it. There is no sense of panic. He takes a step and falls.

I. I. I. I. I.

I see a figure on the overpass.

I don't slow or even think to.

I wonder what he is doing there.

I lean my head toward the breeze.

I hit him as he falls.

I.

And every thing goes white.

There was rain, maybe. Or cool night air with relentless stars, slightly blurred by the acidic glow of lights over the highway. There wasn't much confusion or hubbub. Perhaps a young man related the story hours later at a way station.

A man had fallen from above. He had hit the hood with great force but strangely little sound.

Over shaking coffee cups, two or three wide-eyed strangers nodded their heads and gave comfort to the driver who killed—no, witnessed—the death of a man who fell from above.

He sleeps there in the way station. He gets a room and hangs a DO NOT DISTURB sign on the door. He sleeps like the dead. He had not slept the night before and he sleeps through the whole day. He wakes in the evening and pays the young lady at the counter for the room. He sits down in the diner and orders biscuits and gravy. He thinks it is the best meal he as ever had in his life. He finishes and he goes out to his truck.

Someone has cleaned his truck. Except for a small dent in the hood and front right fender, there is no sign of the collision. He does not recognize anyone in the diner from the day before. He doesn't know if the police have been called. He doesn't care. He gets into his truck, fills it with gas, and begins to drive. He drives through the night. He drives past Chicago and Joliet and Davenport and Des Moines. He stops for gas once. He buys a bag of chips and cigarettes.

When he arrives in Omaha the sun has already risen. It is before noon and he doesn't know where to go. He drives to his grandmother's old house, but someone else is living there now. He sits with the truck running and looks out the window at the house. There is a chain grown into the branches of the locust tree in the front yard. He used to climb that tree. He watched year after year as the chain sunk deeper and deeper into the living wood.

He drives down the block and stops his truck at a park, which is nestled alongside a small creek that runs through the neighborhood. There are children playing on the swings and slides. He gets out of the car and walks across the grass to the playground. There is an empty merry-go-round that he used to play on as a little boy. He lies down on it and closes his eyes.

He takes a breath of the air and it smells familiar. It fills him. He lies there and only breathes. He hears the voices of children approaching. They are whispering at first and quietly closing in. The merry-go-round starts to spin and the voices of the children turn into carefree laughter. It spins faster and faster and the laughter turns into screams of delight. He opens his eyes to see the morning sun spiraling above him.

ACKNOWLEDGMENTS

With the utmost gratitude I want to thank
Susann Suprenant and the engine writers group.
My family for their support, especially my
grandmother for accepting that she isn't
allowed to read this. All my early readers,
especially Shane for the midnight-hour read.
Megan Thomas for an exquisite cover, Chris
Machian for the art shot, Scott Dricky for
the headshot, Darin Jensen for the proof, and
Amazon for enabling the independant spirit.
Kindest regards,

Thom Sibbitt

ABOUT THE AUTHOR

Thom Sibbitt is a Nebraska native. He is the managing director of ætherplough: a tool for cultivating performance in Omaha. He also works as an arts mentor for high school students. Thom has organized writing groups, created original performance work, and facilitated the work of contemporary artists for the last fifteen years.

Thom spent a decade in New York City, where he earned his BFA from New York University, worked extensively in the downtown theater scene, and lost his mind.

In Omaha, Thom gardens, cooks for friends, and works in his woodshop in his infinitesimal free time.